AF208203

IMAGO
DEI
PAUL W.
THOMAS

Copyright © 2022 by Paul Thomas

All rights reserved. No part of this publication may be reproduced, stored or transmitted in any form or by any means, electronic, mechanical, photocopying, recording, scanning, or otherwise without written permission from the publisher. It is illegal to copy this book, post it to a website, or distribute it by any other means without permission.

This novel is entirely a work of fiction. The names, characters and incidents portrayed in it are the work of the author's imagination. Any resemblance to actual persons, living or dead, events or localities is entirely coincidental.

Paul Thomas asserts the moral right to be identified as the author of this work.

Paul Thomas has no responsibility for the persistence or accuracy of URLs for external or third-party Internet Websites referred to in this publication and does not guarantee that any content on such Websites is, or will remain, accurate or appropriate.

Designations used by companies to distinguish their products are often claimed as trademarks. All brand names and product names used in this book and on its cover are trade names, service marks, trademarks and registered trademarks of their respective owners. The publishers and the book are not associated with any product or vendor mentioned in this book. None of the companies referenced within the book have endorsed the book.

First Edition
ISBN: 978-0-578-96008-1
Cover art by Jessica Bell
Typesetting by Jessica Bell

EARTH: THAT WHICH GROUNDS

"On the basis of the Greeks' initial contributions towards an Interpretation of Being, a dogma has been developed which not only declares the question about the meaning of Being to be superfluous but sanctions its complete neglect. It is said that 'Being' is the most universal and the emptiest of concepts."

—Martin Heidegger

WATER: THAT WHICH PERMEATES

"Present human interference with the nonhuman world is excessive, and the situation is rapidly worsening. Policies must therefore be changed. These policies affect basic economic, technological, and ideological structures. The resulting state of affairs will be deeply different from the present."

—Deep Ecology

WIND: THAT WHICH GOVERNS

"Despotism is a legitimate mode of government in dealing with barbarians, provided the end be their improvement, and the means justified by actually effecting that end... but it must be utility in the largest sense, grounded on the permanent interests of man as a progressive being."

—Jonathan Stewart Mill

FIRE: THAT WHICH CONSUMES

"After Buddha was dead, his shadow was still shown for centuries in a cave - a tremendous, gruesome shadow. God is dead; but given the way of men, there may still be caves for thousands of years in which his shadow will be shown. And we—we still have to vanquish his shadow, too."

—Fredrich Nietzsche

SOUL: THAT WHICH ANIMATES

"Cosmos is a Greek word for the order of the universe. It is, in a way, the opposite of Chaos. It implies the deep interconnectedness of all things. It conveys awe for the intricate and subtle way in which the universe is put together."

—Carl Sagan

BEFORE

They came to us in late spring of 2976 AD. Most of our visitors came to the peninsula by boat. Our visitors were always men. So, when the man who called himself Athos arrived with his one-year-old daughter in his arms, most of the brothers were really disturbed.

"Never trust someone who comes by night!" one of them said.

"Jesus himself will come like a thief in the night," I replied.

"But the child? Is it a—"

"It's a girl," Athos interrupted. "She is my daughter, and I would not have come here like this if it weren't an emergency. Please! I am a believer as well. I have nowhere else to go."

The trepidation that night. It was thick on everyone, Athos was afraid, like he was being followed by someone, and the fatigue in his body showed by how he leaned against the wall without regard for how long those walls have stood—more than a thousand years, in fact. But we monks were used to this kind of irreverence. Some of the outsiders would give it a try, but most were sloppy imitators of old ceremonies, even in something as simple as prayer. Most knew to close their eyes, but God forbid there be silence for a time—eyes would open, heads would turn, bodies would shift in anxiety; but of course they would. The world ran away from every tradition by that time till all that was talked about in the public spaces of the world was carbon. The people knew more about carbon than they did about the one who inspired it all.

While the world's sprint away from God and faith was a perpetual grief, I found curiosity in the mystery of Athos's running; whatever it was, he did not share those details, and for some reason I could not escape the thought that either they would be trouble or trouble would find them again. But I also knew that God's love is for all people at all times. Love is usually a discomfort that precedes a greater comfort, and sometimes not everyone shares in that relief. My discomfort started when the child grew out of her toddler years and was nearer to puberty than the cradle. It was the season which I dreaded: the testing of eyes, and flesh, and lust. It was a dread because not everyone on the peninsula had experienced this test before.

There was a brother who was young in the faith, and he showed his measure of self-discipline by his habituated stare, as he would gaze at Anna whenever she took to swimming in the sea. I thought a simple rebuke would end his habit, but her father brought up the issue of Brother Gregory's trespassing eyes yet again. Rebuke turned into a vigilant watch for Anna's well-being, and Gregory went from being a fisherman to a baker overnight. It seemed that it was my responsibility to ensure her safety, as it was my voice that had lifted on their behalf for her stay after all. But it was more than just mere duty or obligation. God seemed to transpose a father's heart in me regarding Anna, and its first pulse was felt during her infant days. One evening during her infancy, Athos required someone to keep her as he bathed himself. As I held her, little Anna reached for a fistful of my beard and plucked several hairs from my face. She was so small then. I never would have anticipated so much vigor in such a tiny hand, and all I could do was laugh. She giggled in return for those hair strings in her kitten-like fist—one of the most precious sounds that ever was.

It wasn't a fair trade, father for mother, but who ever said anything about life being fair? I suppose this instance of fair and not-fair was more in my favor, as I didn't feel life's sting by this exchange. But whatever hurt or ill will had befallen them, I sought to soothe the pain of it by tending to Anna and her father as often as I could. Anna received handmade gifts from me for every birthday, and stories when gathered by an evening fire. Athos received my encouragements from time to time. It was clear he was troubled by something that held fast to him like puppet strings. When he looked gloomy, I would draw him out by conversations about God, as they are endless. He could be found often staring across the sea, watching one of the infamous floating cities being built, and fear would come pouring out of his mouth about it. I would use those moments to remind him about how the Hebrews built Egypt's unholy empire, how they suffered injustice and cruelty while forming every brick of it, and yet God took an enslaved people and made them into a nation, a nation that became a prophet to all the nations—I would speak of hope, faith, and perseverance to him.

I was so preoccupied with assisting Athos in raising Anna that I, soon after their arrival, let them steal all my attention away from the looming global crisis. *Our way of life has survived thousands of years now, and during the rage of many empires, how would this time be any different?* So went my thoughts. But this time would be different. What I didn't realize was that the world had rewritten its story. There was no more, "In the beginning, God created the heavens and the earth." Instead, the world had a different origin story that went something like this: "In the beginning, before Darwin walked away from his god, still further back before Moses walked with his; and still yet preceding when the expanse was taking shape, carbon was—this we know, for the scientist tells us so." There was no telling what kind of ending occurs after such a beginning as that, but I had my suspicions. My mind couldn't resist carbon's elemental make-up in relation to the Infamous Mark. Yet carbon was both protagonist and antagonist to the world, a sort of yin and yang, and therefore could not be made an outright devil, but with its six protons, six neutrons, and six electrons, it liquored the minds of those who were without an origin story. It shook the foundations of belief for everyone else. It was near Anna's eleventh birthday when the peninsula would get its turn to be shaken.

One summer afternoon, without warning, they came on boats. It was like a mighty fleet sailing toward us. They looked like birds gliding over the water, and some had sails that opened above them like great albatross wings. Their ships were many and quick.

I felt the dreadful premonition of death enter my mind and recalled with momentous sentiment the monks at Lindisfarne who were the first to be plundered and killed by the Norsemen. History does, in fact, repeat itself, with or without books, I'm afraid.

When they landed, I expected a thousand Neros to ascend upon us; instead came a Pontius Pilate who questioned the truth of our Christendom and pronounced swift judgement over us—only this time it wasn't by cross that we would suffer but by expelling us indefinitely to a place they called, the "Dead Lands."

ANNA

See the girl with a paintbrush in her hand. Bristled strokes over a rocky canvas trail from her brush. She is painting a woman's face. A familial face. A stranger's face. There is a faint light that pours through the cave she is standing in, for it is early morning. She hears the quiet tide of the sea, feels the growing flame of the sun through crevasses of rock, and if it weren't for her focused brush, she would be awe-swept and gazing. She reminds herself she's seen thousands of sunrises and contents herself in the idea that it will rise again and again, a priori. She doesn't have long. By this time yesterday she only had another thirty minutes before anyone would detect her. Her hand pulls away to study those eyes looking back at her, a blueish hue in the scant light. It is her most recent study and relish of her thoughts. She gawks and ponders on the frame of them, voluptuous arches that meet upon a razor's edge. The woman gives a fatal look, like an exquisite flower with tropical airs hiding grave threats. Could Anna have come from this same pair of eyes? The picture of them was remembered by stolen moments and an excellent memory from which she now transfers this mother's visage. Mother affirmed by good authority, yet the photographed shadows that laid across her face make this cave seem an appropriate venue to exhibit this femme fatale. Occasionally, Anna practices calling aloud to the image, "Mother," thinking that perhaps then she would feel a kindred spirit, but her voice just disappears into the cave.

See the man cradling a photograph in his hand. It's a picture of her, the blue-eyed woman. He caresses her face with the pillow of his thumb. He studies her with intense eyes—eyes like Michelangelo's *David*; pensive, somewhere between thought and action. The man looks like a giant killer too, but he promised her he would never give in to the revolution, or worse, contend it. While promises are as delicate as thread, women have a way with men—turning warriors into poets. Many wonderful customs are born out of women's demand for civility. Take away all womankind and a nasty sort of brutish life awaits. Those seemingly frivolous and impractical pleasantries—fresh-cut flowers, bottled perfumes, jewelry, and the like—are but the nerve-endings of feminine soul that require a civil breeze. The inclination for beautiful things is not vanity but artwork curated by Her soul. "Polite society," as it may be called, is how She can manifest all her art. He had promised his woman a life of contentment despite the Free World's "Goliath" roaming freely, but that promise would fill his mouth like a dirty word. His only tether to it now is the memory caught in his hands. With whispered thoughts to her ghost, and God also, he mutters, "What have I done?"

She wants to sign her name below the image, but she knows she can't. She's already trespassed against the Free World and its laws governing the arts. Laws as such:

No artist shall embroider, decorate, garnish, paint, sculpt, draw, or
design the image of homo-sapiens in ANY biome.
No art shall be imbued with authorial or creator designation.

So instead, she leans close to the cave wall and breathes her name on the rock, "Anna." The earth would know whose art adorns her. A humble signature of carbon dioxide where two witnesses of oxygen atoms for every molecule can attest: Anna did indeed paint her mother's face. The Free World has yet to learn the secret language of molecules, and so their testaments will remain as monad gibberish.

Anna turns to gather her belongings, and that's when she notices a spider preying in its web. Some poor insect is about to have its last moments, and Anna is fixated on this arachnid scene. The little bug is desperate, squirming and flexing. The spider waits as if it knows time is on its side. The bug relents and gives pause, and in that second the arthropod flings itself toward the bug with fangs bared. Anna winces.

The air is ripe with spring pollen; voices are carried over the aeolian breeze, and their words seem just as archaic. Anna hears the voices softly pouring into the cave, the sound of the Thrushes. They are a coveted select few, a sort of elected choir designated to sing upon sunrise and sunset. They come in groups of three. They are scattered about the peninsula where there are Dasein habitats. They act as biological clocks and mystics singing blessing over the earth. As sisters three, they sing. Sometimes they sing about the seasons changing, sometimes about the living things, great and small. Their sound is as folk, and their voices are braided together in the manner of sirens singing a cappella. The honesty in their voices utters vulnerability; they sound delicate in their range of emotion. Sometimes hypnotic. Sometimes as one, sometimes as three, but always about the earth, they sing.

Anna, realizing she should be leaving now, lingers in the cave to gaze at her work. It is uncouth for anyone to be up before dawn and interfering with grazing animals, let alone dwelling upon such subjects of art as hers. Each second is like a wave swelling in size and coming straight for her, but she stands still anyway. She imagines what a world it would be if men and women existed once again; if God could be raised from the tomb of society's mouth—what a world it might be … but her thoughts splintered upon impact with a male Dasein voice that yelled through the air. Anna peeked through a blind of trees to see if it was him, and it was. There, about half a kilometer away. Time to go.

Anna finishes stuffing her bag with all her art things and peeks out of the cave to see if anyone else is on the shore yet. She cautions herself by lifting the hood of her greenish cloak over her head of golden-saffron, for it is just as rare too. She is the only one who wears a head of reddish hair, which privately makes her uneasy. It makes her stand out. Everywhere she goes people know it is her without inquiry. Even all of the time spent in the sun cannot dim her natural color enough to better blend in. And so, she cannot compromise herself or have her cave found. She clutches her bag tightly as she goes, looking over her shoulder the whole way home.

The world is one that now pines to outlive the oldest stars and think it possible. The survivors of what is commonly called "The Old World War" by the elders who remember the world as it was have outlived the radicalism of the religious, the patriotism of the nationalists, and the moral imperatives of the pious. All of these fell as titans before a progressive, Western-thinking body-politic that had languished under the Anthropocene Era (A.E.) long enough. Time's umbrella now opens as (B.E.): The Biocene Era.

This era began on September 22, 2971; however, the official manner of expressing that date would be Mustumarious 22, 2971 B.E. The months also changed under the Eco Calendar. They are:

Pluviary

Glaciary

Buddal

Floreal

Pratum

Reapido

Heatidor

Metodor

Mustumarious

Caliguous

Geluious

Ninguous

Time has always been B.C. – A.D. for Anna's father. His world-view and its division of epochs was presented to him by his father, in such a way that he knew he would pass on the traditions of a creature in awe of their creator, likewise, by love. But these traditions are only secrets now.

What was once a socially acceptable dogma has become as wine vinegar in the mouth of the public. Such contentious division led to war; war inspired Athos to run with his daughter, and he traveled, thenceforth, under a new name. He fled from Thessaloniki to seek refuge from the monks that resided on Mount Athos. It was perhaps a bit presumptuous to assume the name of the place he required so much of, but he trusted that the monks would oblige by imitating their creator, by showing mercy.

When the day is hard, he thinks of Father Stephanos. A debt of gratitude is continuously paid to the memory of him. Athos leaned on him almost like one parent does to the other in the trying moments of parenting. It wasn't a role Athos bestowed or that Father Stephanos offered, but it was a role he assumed by accepting Anna's curious interest in him. Athos always marveled at the bond between his daughter and Father Stephanos; occasionally, Athos even grew jealous of it. Father Stephanos would come to the door of their room and Anna would leap from Athos's lap and run to greet him. There were times when Anna pined for stories from Father Stephanos rather than from her own father, and this would upset him enough to encourage him to take long walks while Anna delighted in Father Stephanos's stories. He looks back to those moments now with regret. He would rather share his role as friend and mentor with Father Stephanos than to have witnessed his daughter's cries. He saw that Anna adored Father Stephanos like a granddaughter adores her pappouli.

There isn't much that Athos concedes to the Free World, he's just good at hiding it. He hides the past with the photo of the blue-eyed woman; concealed and secret, it stays. The picture lays between the thin leaves and thick cover of a leatherbound book like a bookmark. When he is alone, he uncovers this most prized possession in order to keep his mind trained on the musings of long-ago sages and sinners. He lingers on the words of those Pauls and Peters and Pontius Pilates and Pharos. Their questions and conclusions rattle his bones righteous, turning his spine straight as an exclamation point. Such dangerous certainty is his ethos and legacy for his daughter. And yet, it is in those private moments that his thoughts might reveal a kinship with King David's wandering eye: the lingering stare he gave to the photographed woman—a Bathsheba staring back at him. Athos doesn't want his daughter to see him so vulnerable for such a volcanic love, an unvirtuous love, a villainous love. Thus, Athos's Bathsheba hides in that leather, bound between Psalms and Isaiah.

If only he knew that Anna had already found his secret hiding place, he wouldn't have to go through so much trouble.

He's sitting on the second floor of his home because that's where the foliage begins to thicken on the tree, and what he does is less noticeable. Like Adam in the Garden he hides, thinking the picture of his sin has never been seen.

Their home is like all the other Dasein homes: rotund, cylindrical, and built around a single tree. The tree is precious in the Free World, and just because things like houses require wood doesn't make them less so. A house is as tall as the tree it was built around. They are at least two-storied. Athos's is five. Floors second and higher consist of glass in order to let in sunlight, as is custom for all households. The limbs and leaves of the house trees may be pruned in order to make way for home-living, but prudence is necessary in this. There is a sort of mutual contract between Dasein and tree. The Dasein protect the life of the tree, and the living situation of the Dasein is protected in return. Should the tree begin to rot and die, the home would be repossessed by the authorities and most likely recycled into whatever carbon they deemed appropriate. Therefore, it is in every Dasein's best interest to maintain the life of the tree, for the tree's life is their life.

Anna comes pouring through the front door like a gust of wind. Athos quickly looks up at the leaves, which flexed in the change of air pressure. He wipes his eyes after rewrapping the leather book in old-world plastic and pushing it onto a leafy branch.

"Anna?" He stands and peers down the spiraling staircase to see her still wearing her hood. "Where have you been?" She pauses in her steps upward and slowly pulls her hood off as if collecting her thoughts.

"Out."

"Oh?" he says shifting his weight, annoyed by her brevity.

"Just, out," is all she can say.

She continues up the staircase toward her room, but Athos side-steps in front of her and crosses his arms. It is evident to him that she was rushing away for some mysterious reason, panting for breath as she is, but he has secrets of his own that he, only seconds ago, had stepped away from. *Stalemate*, he thinks.

"Penguin" he says with a straight face.

"Papa, please! Don't do this, not now."

"Penguin" he says, only this time with his lips curling into a grin.

"Papa, stop!"

"Penguin," his grin now turned full smile.

"Picasso!" she snorts back and slips past her father.

Athos's smile summits into a laugh, the same laugh he'd given when he first heard his daughter refer to him as Picasso. He had initially taken offense. He doesn't like Picasso. He doesn't like Picasso's use of the color blue and champions El Greco's work over his; to have Athos's daughter refer to him and the painting he was working on at the time as a "Picasso" made him laugh. He had laughed the same way when Anna was being taught how to swim. She was on a rock, not very high above the water, but high enough to scare a little girl. She stood on that rock for about twenty minutes until giving in to her father's prompt and she "belly-flopped like a penguin," as her papa described it that day. He never let her forget it either. She's been "his little penguin" ever since he's been her Picasso.

Anna works in the Par Terre garden while her father works in the vineyard and saffron field. She helps to curate a place for Dasein to enthrall themselves before the comeliness of the earth, while her father contents himself to support the biome's exports of crops. They are good at their jobs, and the earth is made more lovely because of them, but today is a day for reprieve.

Anna lies in her bed. She turns on her side and looks out through the glass wall before her. Her father made sure that the floor plans of their home would favor Anna, granting her a room toward the top so that she could have a view of those afflatus-born skies, while his was a practical choice on the second floor—residing between Anna and the world.

She's trying to calm herself down from her morning's thrill. She is gazing out from the fourth floor at the treetops marshaled together like clouds before a rainfall, sinuous and plump. She's looking southeast, away from the peninsula and toward the climbing sun. She remembers what her father said about light. "It is art itself; without it, there *is* no art." It struck her funny when she was little, but with each day dawning she believes him more and more. The sun unveils the manifold shades of the sea, from emerald to crystallite, the tapioca sands laying like a nude painted by the sun. The pastel skies empty, not a cloud cleaving. She gazes at this fading masterpiece for as long as she can, ignoring the far-off floating city cast in shadow. It is inevitable. She cannot help, but to look at it all, the city on the water too. From where she lies, she can only see its shape, but it bothers her like a sky full of clouds.

She remembers the day when the place she called home for her first ten years there would be rebranded as Biome 1, for it was counted as the first spear of the three Greek peninsulas jutting out into the Aegean Sea in the shape of a trident. When the boats arrived, they came from that city, and they took Father Stephanos away from her while Anna and her father remained because of a lie that they were only tourists permitted by a bribe. She knows she will come undone if she sits and looks too long at the city. She would remember Father Stephanos, about how he cared for her and she for him.

It is a city to be seen as "a beacon of progress" with all of its symmetry, its sustainable features, and all by the mighty hand of a globalized effort. Its glory stands arrogantly before Anna, as if a new world tower of Babel. Its grandeur is not so aesthetically neat to Anna as to cheat the idea of a great and utopian civilization—they have just as much blood on their hands as any mass murdering tyrant.

She rolls over to find a better view. She must look past the branches of the tree that grows in the house if she is to see outside. She moves her head up, then down. There's a branch jutting out in her line of sight. It isn't a very strong branch. She could snap it off if she wants. And why shouldn't she?

Anna rolls back over with a tear trekking along the bridge of her nose. She can't shake Stephanos's ghost after all. She can't forget the life she had before the Dasein arrived. It was free from the rigid living she must now oblige. The earth now seems a delicate place, and a place that deserves a posture next to worship according to the Dasein. All Anna wants is the human dignity she once knew; instead, she suffers the bombardment of Dasein rhetoric with the tree that grows in the middle of the house. Many regard this architectural requirement as necessary and revolutionary, but Anna only sees limbs and leaves getting in the way of her thoughts, poking at her face with indifference.

She looks out the other direction and sees one of the old monasteries in ruins. The walls around it, once upright and level, now look like broken teeth. Some parts of them even missing whole teeth altogether. It stands abandoned with only the haunt of vegetation. A single tree stands taller than the rest of the greenery; taller than the monastery itself. Anna fixates on the tree. Its enormous size casts a shadow over the ill-fated halidom. Anna tries to imagine the sound and content of prayers that must have echoed there, but all she can hear are the whispers of photosynthesis.

She turns over once again, and in a temper, snaps off the tree limb that protrudes into her line of sight, and then lies on her back with a slight smile. She has defied the Free World with a single squeeze in a single second. She feels like she did in the cave—passionate, alive, but burdened. The Free World is a place full of beauty to indulge in, but there are codified ways in which to do so. One does not adore in any which way; there are limitations, bulwarks that keep every Dasein from exceeding undue effect or injury to the earth. But the world does little to keep injury from her. Who is to pay for the crime against her?

See her scar: a blotchy pattern of reddish flesh that skirts her right eye. The scalding heat closed in just enough to take part of her outer eyebrow, for hair no longer grows there. Its presence is never shown. Few Dasein actually know that she has the scar. She is so self-conscious of the scar by her eye that she is startled when someone identifies the green in *both* of her eyes. If eyes are a topic of discussion, she would rather dismiss it altogether. Her scar is a ghoul that creeps into her thoughts, always found in the recesses of her mind. She covers it with her long curly hair like a veil; but like veils, this has an unwanted effect: they present themselves like twin sisters—Mystery and Tease. Soon stares will not be enough for her admirers, and she and her father know it. It's why, together, they have lied about her age. She's been 21 going on 18 for almost a year now, and she knows this deceit cannot continue.

THE WORLD WITHOUT GOD

There is no God when there are no "people." Instead, there is only Dasein. To be a Dasein is to be a being, and every being has materialized in a unique place within the space-time continuum, and that reality is to be honored like cells in the body: individually important but part of a greater whole. The Free World does not extrapolate some sort of identity and confer it upon its citizenry. Each Dasein must decide for themselves what kind of Dasein they wish to be, but like all good things, there is a catch.

Like Furies unleashed, the Dasein came with iconoclastic purpose: to supplant all evidence of religious token and symbol. When the Free World grew fully conscious of the hermitages on Mount Athos and its congress of men, of orthodoxy, of its archaic arrangement of carbon in the shape of crosses, it was altogether seen as appalling. The Dasein came to a consensus that all religion was guilty of bad faith, that both founders and acolytes were in league to subdue and enslave humanity and the natural world with it. At the very minimum, religion was said to limit the way humanity could live. The Dasein were willing to evolve beyond the reaches of "thou shall" and "thou shall not." For this reason, Anna now hides her soul from society.

The next morning, she is already at it again. Anna takes to the brush like a thief. A slow, steady, creeping walk is her pace. She looks like a cat stalking her prey. Her father had trained her to have a careful attention to her surroundings. When she is alone, she is to keep an eye out for predators, as there are no more fenced-in nature preserves—all of the natural world has become one large nature preserve. When she looks to the sky, she is to pay attention to the flight of the birds, and especially when they perch in the trees. She knows to do this from her father. She remembers his warning about the birds: "Even in your thoughts, do not curse the king, nor in your bedroom curse the rich, for a bird of the air will carry your voice, or some winged creature tell the matter. Do you know what I mean by this?" her father had asked. But words like 'king' and 'rich' are mostly concepts to Anna. Her father had offered another axiom: "Pluck a swan of all its feathers and you'll have a bald goose. Don't you see?" he asked, "Perception is everything now."

Anna laughed at her father's newfound proverb, and the featherless goose became the joke between them for a while. It wasn't until he made explicit the very real threat against them that she understood his warning was real. He made sure to speak about it further in private.

He spoke of drones in the shape of birds.

"Watch what you say when you go about the peninsula. If you must talk about God or to God, look first. If you see them, then whisper," he'd said.

Anna doesn't remember when she started whispering in the presence of birds. To her, it feels like something she's always done since the time of the Dasein. Whenever a bird flies nearby, she stops to watch it. She studies its head movements, like her father taught her, to see whether they will bob up and down or gawk at her from eye to eye. The drones seem less capable to imitate the rapid head bobbing and careening at the neck, no matter how much biomimicry they exhibited. Her father suggested that it must have been too difficult a trait for the operator to manage while conducting their surveillance and therefore the drones would merely gawk at them instead. Her father taught her to look for the birds that perch and linger on the trees and never come down to scrape their beaks along the earth looking for food. The birds of prey also. It didn't matter. If a bird is watching them, they are to whisper.

Anna places each step so as to avoid excessive noise from the rocks beneath her. She looks out to the sea to make sure there's not a single boat making way for the peninsula. She watches the sky like a hawk watches the ground. She is confident to approach her cave, and it's only a dozen more paces now between her and her private sanctum. She stops and listens before going farther. She takes a final look at the nearby treetops. All is clear.

"Anna? Are you hungry?" asks Athos.

Silence resounds throughout the house.

Athos is stirring in the kitchen—kitchens are usually structured toward the base of the tree, as is theirs, and from it, Athos calls upward to Anna's bedroom, but there is no answer.

"She's done it again, hasn't she?"

Athos suspects that she has gone off; she's made a habit of sneaking off in the mornings, so he doesn't bother to look upstairs. It normally wouldn't matter, but Athos is ignoring a fear that grows in the pit of him with each passing day.

The date is fast approaching—his daughter is expected to participate in the coming-of-age ceremony, and he can delay it no longer. To the Dasein, it is an exalting moment in one's life—an adolescent turned adult—but the occasion hints at something else. It puts the newly recognized adults on display to include them in the summer celebration of Kípos.

Kípos is a time to celebrate the world between its bloom and harvest, to delight in the fertile grounds of the biome. It is also a time to facilitate a new adult's first, or "official," sexual experience. It is considered safe this way, to provide a place to nurture an appetite for it and to exercise a confidence for the occasion. Athos counts the occasion as ungodly, and he has been sure to let Anna know as much. He regards it as an abrupt intrusion on the intentions of God: sex is to be enjoyed in the safe place of marriage between a man and a woman, not as a shared and communal activity prompted by momentary lust—a conviction that is now troubled by a difficult and personal history.

Athos cannot escape his past. Anna's very existence is the biproduct of his own sexual sin. All these years later, and he still sees the wrinkle upon his conscience. When the Spring festival comes, he is uneasy to say the least. The subject matter of everyone's thoughts turn to sex such that the peninsula looks to flowers and herbs to find the next aphrodisiac; meanwhile Athos secludes himself from their activity. Chopping firewood is his usual go-to habit to distract himself from the eroticism that lingers thickly in the air. It is only recently that Athos realized he has also secluded Anna from any real conversations about sex, and soon she is to make an important decision about it. *What boundary lines will she decide?* he wonders.

Anna spends about a half-hour sanding by candlelight the next bit of rock wall she intends to paint. It is a menial task, but she knows it has to be done. She loses herself to the cadence of scratching against the surface until her hands cramp.

One day, Anna had found an oval-shaped gap in the cave that allowed light in, and she relies on this gap to tell the time. She always performs her prep in the final reaches of early morning twilight and gives herself no more than a half-hour after sunrise for painting. It isn't a perfect situation because the Thrushes aren't as systematic. They are more religious about the content of their songs than the exact timing of them. Anna has not accounted for the fact that sunrise now occurs earlier in the morning, and there is no real telling when the Thrushes will rise.

The Free World seems to pour all of its contempt of the old world onto Mount Athos. Because of the former occupants and the quality of their convictions, seemingly impervious to time, the Free World has filled the peninsula's new vacancy with a zealous fraction of a female to male population by a four-to-one ratio. So, it is not uncommon for Anna to meet other female Dasein more frequently wherever she goes. It is, however, irregular for anyone to meet any of the Thrushes before they sing at the start of the day. Anna has just left her cave, and not five minutes later, she runs into one.

"Anna? What are you doing out here?"

A tall female form stands before Anna, garbed in the custom white tunic, and upon her head, a floral crown that every member wears.

"Oh, uh … hi, Zoe. I was—"

"You know you're not supposed to be outside yet."

Anna is startled. She doesn't know when Zoe actually first saw her. Anna can only think of her cave, which makes her tongue lifeless in her mouth. She has nothing, no lie, no pretense, just a guilty face.

"Well?" Zoe prods.

Anna still has no words.

"I am an obligatory reporter, you know this, don't you?"

Zoe gives a condescending tone, which sparks an anger in Anna that can only be seen in her now-tense brows. Anna is almost 18 years old to Zoe and to the rest of the peninsula. Not yet an adult. Zoe doesn't know they are actually the same age, and from this ignorance she speaks: "Mother will be displeased to find out about this."

"Ah, there she is!" Athos's voice comes barreling over Zoe's shoulder.

"Well, if it isn't Athos, the hermit. Look at this, both of you out during curfew."

Athos, now realizing the situation, quickly provides the pretense.

"I sent Anna to go get some sand for a home-improvement project."

"Sand? You really expect me to believe that?"

"Yes! That's what I was doing," says Anna abruptly. But a lie always sounds like a lie when you are trying to convince someone without having been convinced of it yourself.

"The sand is to make a mortar," Athos doubles down on his lie.

Zoe looks at Athos, then back at Anna.

"If she is fetching sand for you, how is she to collect it? I don't see a bucket or anything on either one of you."

Anna speaks up; it is her turn to have another go at the pretense.

"I forgot the bucket, actually. I was going back to get it."

Anna proceeds to walk back toward their home, and Athos turns as well until Zoe speaks up again.

"Hey Athos, next time, fetch your own dirt. There are no hand-maidens here." The muscles in Zoe's face twist with contempt with her last remark.

Athos hides his frustration in his cheek, which is now pinched between his teeth, and walks away with a quickened stride.

They had yet to reach the porch of their home when Athos can no longer contain his fear, and he lets it come out as anger.

"Anna! What were you doing out there?"

"Nothing. I was just enjoying the morning air," she says with a wave of her hands.

"Anna, don't lie to me! After all, you're not a good liar."

"No, not as good as you father," Anna snaps back sarcastically.

"Anna! Hold on a minute."

But Anna stomps up the porch and into the house.

"Anna! Please! Listen, I'm sorry," is the only way her father can beckon her.

Anna stops just before the staircase to her room, turning to face her father to hear what is so important to him.

"Anna … I love you. I don't want us to fight like this. I just wanted to have breakfast with my daughter this morning, that's all." He gives her a warm look, and she lets it relax the defensive posture she's been holding. She uncrosses her arms and leans on the stair post while fidgeting with the ends of her hair.

"Zoe said that she was going to report me," Anna says, "that she would inform the Mother."

"Don't call her that! She is nobody's mother. She's hardly a mother to her own child, and she wants everyone here to go around with 'Mother' on their lips? And then she goes and sleeps with whomever she pleases? What a sick joke! Mother … call her Sybil, and nothing else." Her father shuffles into the kitchen to prepare some eggs for the two of them.

"Mother," he scoffs.

Anna's contempt for Sybil is partially loaned to her from her father, but a part of her wishes for a mother, somebody who can better understand the parts of her that her father can't. Some days, she thinks it would be better to at least have a Sybil for a mother than to not have a mother at all.

Her father is there to remind her of her soul and its tether to God—a reality that is not shared by the Dasein. The reality of sex, desire, and the swirl of chemistry that moves by the cadence of blood and by the rhythm of the warm air between two bodies is a reality for both Dasein and man, for the unbeliever and the believer. Yet this has not been a conversation between them, and it leaves curiosity burning inside her.

Curiosity has never had a face for Anna to lust after. There were no male Dasein her age until recently. When the peninsula first opened up for newcomers, it was mostly female Dasein looking for refuge from war-torn countries or to flee male abusers. Eventually, male Dasein came as well. They began to arrive soon after the poppies started to bloom. The preeminence of the female Dasein presence was first noticed by analysts and traders sailing nearby those shores after the orange blooms took hold of the peninsula. After being transplanted there with the female Dasein, they bloomed wild across the mountainside. The earth seemed to welcome them both as a rapturous host. The poppy embraced the biome's carbon like a scandalous affair caught aflame while the female Dasein stoked the fires of their newfound freedoms however they wished. Together, they roused under the sun as modestly as a summer dress pulled above the waist.

Anna has heard of the reasons why sex is dangerous. It was a brief lesson made awkward by her father after she told him about seeing a female Dasein naked with a male Dasein. He promised her that with sex comes scabs, sores, and puss. A more gratuitous lesson from him might have included the fire metaphor: that it is better to put a fire in the fireplace, than to let it loose in a forest. Anything instead of his now tight-lipped demeanor would have been better for Anna, for other voices would flirt ideas within the void of his silence.

Several years ago, and on a hot afternoon, one of the other girls Anna tended the gardens with, Cleo, asked if she would like to go with her to her favorite spot to swim. Anna said yes. They'd spent hours under the sun already, and the fastest way to cool down was a dip in the sea. They ran to the edge of the emerald waters, and Anna was prepared to immediately jump in, but Cleo halted Anna before her toes could spring under her leap.

"Wait!" said Cleo. "What about your clothes? Aren't you going to take them off first?"

Anna felt the question a tad off-putting. She hadn't swum with anybody since she was very young. It was a routine learned from the days when the monks still lived on the peninsula: if she were to swim, it was with her clothes on.

"Bad habit," said Anna.

She turned away slowly to hide her embarrassment. She became aware of her shyness such that her embarrassment was itself embarrassing. She was fumbling over her fingers to get her clothes off, when she heard Cleo prodding her on.

"What are you waiting for? Come on!" Cleo said as she plunged into the cool sea.

Cleo was someone with perfect olive skin, and she knew as much, for there was already, at fifteen, an enthusiasm of male Dasein fingers tracing over her.

Anna looked on with amusement and a smile. The delight of a midday swim was all over Cleo's face. She was naked and free, and the joy in her smile was for no other moment. Anna wondered if she could feel the same way.

Anna would jump in, but she waited until Cleo submerged herself and couldn't see just how pale Anna's skin gets. Anna was surprised by how much pleasure she got from skinny dipping that afternoon, but it would be the only occasion she enjoyed with Cleo.

That same year, when the air was turning crisp and the emerald waters were better to look at than to swim in, a world of sexuality began to unmask itself before Anna. She was invited by Cleo to join her and some friends during the celebration of the Harvest Moon. A courtyard fire blazed inside the perimeter of shadowy dancers and merry revelers, all of them under the influence of a very large, amber-filled moon and this year's vintage. Anna took advantage of her father's decided absence of the occasion and whisked herself away with Cleo while her father found a convenient need for chopping firewood. Cleo promised Anna a night to explore one of the abandoned monasteries nearby, but her company had other plans.

When Anna met Cleo by the monastery she spoke about, she arrived and found several other Dasein boys and girls circled around a fire of their own. Their laughter ripped through the air after every heckle and joke from the boys, and the girls leaned on them and danced about as their liquored moods fancied. Anna approached them timidly until Cleo called out to her.

"There she is! Hey, girl, where have you been?" asked Cleo.

Lexical boys and girls survived the purging of "man" and "woman." Somehow, a "girl" didn't become a woman; one of the few relics of the old world.

Anna began to respond, but before she could answer one of the other girls spoke out—

"Oh good, now we have even numbers. We're just getting ready to play a game. You stand over here," said the girl.

Anna was to stand between two boys, as did the other girls, all in boy-girl-order.

"What are we playing?" asked Anna shyly.

"Truth or Dare!" shouted one of the boys.

"I've never played this game," said Anna.

"I bet there's other games you haven't played yet either," said one of the boys, chuckling.

Anna was too naïve to begin to know what he meant by 'other games,' and her silence only encouraged their teenage wit further. Anna would have been okay to leave them, then and there, but before she could reason to do so, Cleo huffed at them.

"Leave her alone. She came to have fun."

One of the other girls introduced herself as a kind gesture and elaborated on the game.

"Hi Anna, I'm Cassi. All right, so Truth or Dare, it's a game of secrets or bravery, nothing else to it. What do you say?"

"Okay," said Anna, feeling a bit coaxed into the unknown.

"Look, we'll give you a trial run. Truth or dare?"

"What?"

"Truth or dare? Pick one," said Cassi.

"Truth."

"Let's do an easy one. How old are you?" asked Cassi.

"Thirteen," said Anna.

"Thirteen! Oh, you young thing," Cassi remarked.

One of the boys howled her age out of his mouth and it rung in Anna's ears.

But this was a lie, of course, as Anna was older than most of them there. If it weren't for her less-rounded features and lack of confidence, perhaps she would be the bad liar her father said she was, but she was taught this lie. She accepted this lie, and sometimes it was to her benefit. She was already regretting this game.

Cleo was to take the first official turn in choosing a truth to tell or a dare to do. She chose a dare. Anna couldn't believe the sudden turn in the game—it had only begun! It was startling to witness what so few rules could allow. Cleo was to pull her top off for everyone to gaze at her and then pass her top to the Dasein that was next to her to signify whose turn it was.

Felix was his name. Felix stood between Anna and Cleo, which made Anna nervous because there was no telling how the game would evolve.

Felix also chose dare over truth, and he was dared to grab Cleo's boobs, which he did. Anna couldn't decide what was more startling: the fact that Felix so willingly reached and lingered with his hands or that Cleo stood there with her hands on her waist and a smirk on her face. Anna looked around at everyone and saw that no one there was perturbed in the least; meanwhile Anna felt like hiding behind her hair. Laughter ensued, jokes went around, and eyes flirted between Cleo's neck and navel. Anna sensed that Cleo ate up all the attention she was getting. She was naked and free, and the joy in her smile was for no other moment. Cleo's shirt was passed to Anna.

"Anna, you're up," said Cassi, who had assumed the role of game host.

Anna's heart began to throb.

"Truth or dare?" asked Cassi, but there was silence.

"Oh no, you don't get to skip," said Cassi.

Some of the others gave suggestions to her. The male Dasein were shouting, "Dare," while Anna recoiled at the thought of either.

"Fine," said Cassi, "let's do it this way: truth—you tell us whether or not you are a virgin; dare—you have to kiss Felix for one minute in front of everyone. What'll it be?"

Anna was mortified. The ultimatum felt like they were picking at her age, a false age, yet the truth of her sixteen years didn't make it any better. It would have been counted a greater thing to lampoon a sixteen-year-old, but what was decided as acceptable harassment of a thirteen-year-old was uncomfortable already.

"Oh come on!" griped one of the male Dasein.

"Don't be a prude," another hounded.

The more they beckoned, the more Anna wanted to run. If it were daylight out, all would have seen the embarrassment flush over her pale skin.

"I don't think this game is for me," said Anna.

Everyone hollered their disapproval at Anna's rejection until the game host intervened.

"Quiet, all of you! If she doesn't want to play, then she doesn't have to ... the sweet thing," said Cassi. At this, all of the Dasein roared with laughter and were appeased by Cassi's backhanded comment about Anna.

"All right, next," said Cassi, and the Dasein next to Anna was to take on a dare. "I dare you to go into this monastery," said Cassi pointing to the darkened building behind her, "and you must go by yourself, and bring back something with you."

The Dasein agreed with enthusiasm and entered where the door once was. He walked into the dark portal of everyone's imagination. It was curious enough of a thing to tempt Anna to remain in their company a bit longer as she wondered what the Dasein would bring back. After a long ten minutes, he was lost to the wild ideas in everyone's heads. Some joked that he'd been snatched up by a monk that never left the peninsula, while others complained that he was taking too long, until they all heard foot-steps rushing toward them. When he walked back through the doorway, however, he didn't bring anything back.

"You all have to come check this out. Follow me," he said, and everyone followed.

Anna dragged her hands along the hallway to prevent herself from falling. The air was cold and earthy and gave off the smell of wasted pottery long forgotten. The noise of each Dasein voice echoed throughout the halls. They recycled between scaring each other and laughing at themselves, and for a moment, the darkness didn't seem as terrible as it appeared.

"This better be good," said Cleo.

"Are you scared?" asked Cassi.

"No, but I'm getting cold," said Cleo sharply.

"Come here, I'll keep you warm," said Felix with a chuckle.

"Shh, quiet! Look! There it is."

Anna filed behind the others into a room from which a singular glow emanated. A lone candle stood propped up on a stone on the floor, and there were more stones surrounding it with intent, by design. They were spread out into lines, which became points, and some lines intersected others until the shape of a five-pointed star appeared.

"Someone set this up. Someone is here," said one of the male Dasein.

"Look at the wax," said Cassi, "it's been dripping for a while."

"Yeah, but who would have put this here?" asked another.

"I bet I know who … It's her," said Felix.

"You mean the witch?" asked another.

"Well, of course I do," said Felix.

"She is not a witch!" Cassi chided. "She is a priestess and nothing less."

They all stared at the flame, how petite it was, and yet it commanded the attention of everyone in that room. The mystery of the witch, of the priestess, was churning in their thoughts until Cassi seemed to find the resolve that everyone wanted.

"Hey, so if this was set up by the priestess, I don't think she would appreciate our messing with it. We should leave."

Anna left the company of her harassers once she found the flames of the bonfire, which still leaped together. She walked toward the light of the fire and then headed home. There was much that attended her thoughts. She felt embarrassment and shame; meanwhile, a reproachful and curious streak of attitude accompanied her.

How could Cleo set me up like that? Cassi was more of a friend than Cleo was, and what a bunch of perverts, went Anna's thoughts. She thought about how there was more than her soul that she would have to conceal, if she were to keep her secret from the likes of the Felix's about the peninsula. It wasn't until she felt the air in her lungs moving rapidly from her brisk walk home that she began to think about the witch, the 'priestess' as Cassi called her. Whatever she was, whatever she was doing, she was out there in the dark, and Anna didn't want to be out in it any longer.

THE WORLD WITHOUT RELIGION

His name is Howard Phillips, and like all the others, he, too, is a transplant to Biome 1; but he is not like the others. He is a scientist. He is *the* scientist and liaison between Biome 1 and the region's floating city. He's a biologist who's been seen as having promise to work upon one of the floating cities where, in his mind, *the really interesting stuff happens.* There, scientists monitor the entire biosphere. A biome is complex, but entire regions and the biosphere itself is "the pro-leagues." To be bumping elbows with the world's greatest minds is a daydream for Howard, but there is something else that occurred at these cities that spikes his heart rate into what the layman would call 'hope.' There, they have been configuring methodology and the means to colonize other planets. The truth is, Howard possesses no hope in the Dasein, specifically the "land dwellers," as he calls them. "There's still humanity in them," he says. He never trusted humanity before the war, and he doesn't trust them now. His knowledge of psychology is vested in a book he once read by the now-antiquated William James, and he has never forgotten what Mr. James said about "people of faith." Howard keyed in on the two kinds of people Mr. James spoke of, and it all made perfect sense to him.

Howard fancies himself a "tough-minded" Dasein, while the other land dwellers he thinks of as "tender-minded" Dasein and the prime object of his observations.

It isn't enough to monitor the flora and fauna of the biome. The Dasein need monitoring as well. In Howard's mind, if there is any lesson to be had from the Anthropocene Era, it is that humans not only affect one another, but they effect the entire biosphere, and rarely is it for the good.

"The good." Such a curious phrase for the tough-minded Howard. He doesn't believe in good or evil—such ideas are "the stuff of fairytales and fiction," he says. What he does believe in is the magic of the bee. He keeps several hives on shore, just below a tree line, and he begins each morning by minding his own bees before he monitors the peninsula. This practice usually takes him about an hour. An hour to walk on land. An hour to pretend that he is a man (in the old-world sense) and that he's back at his native English home in Canterbury. He pretends for a moment that he's leaving the coast to return to Kent, where he'll meet friends at the ol' Saddler for a drink. *Hell, any pub'll do,* he thinks. The humming of bees takes him out of his daydream as easily as it slinks him into it.

The bees are as close as Howard likes to get to the Dasein. He returns to a ringlike structure that straddles the shore. Its black roof is an all-weather sun panel. Parts of the ring show the inside by way of windows, and from there light emits in the evenings. The circular glow upon the water makes it look as though a space-ship has landed and some extraterrestrial exchange seemingly to promise that of a Napoleon figure would emerge only to be met by a sort of Hugo challenge: pitiful. Yet, pity is not a requisite impulse for Howard's position. The three judges of the biome often referred to him as, "the Dublican." He interacts with the judges only when necessary, for they too are "tender-minded" by Howard's estimation. In fact, he would place blame at their feet for propagating the old world and allowing it to prosper.

This trinity of judges weigh in on matters of trespasses against the Dasein of Biome 1 and trespasses against all the matorral organisms. The sacred duty of the Dasein is to act like enzymes of the earth, stimulating growth and harmony across the trophic levels in the carbon cycle—this the Dublican respects, but the judges also allow the Dasein their "spiritual fancies," as he calls it. Despite outlawing religion across the world, the Dasein on Biome 1 have leaned into the earth's gravity and still found religion.

But not even the Dublican can rid the old world out of himself, and perhaps his greatest virtue is his knack for self-reflection: He knows that he has flirted with Napoleonic ideas. Ideas like scourging the peninsula of all the land dwellers and transplanting only scientists loyal to the entire biosphere—that's a weekly fancy.

The morning has come. The photons currently warming Anna in her cave neighbor beside the photons that come down on Howard's slicked back, dirty-blonde head. The Dublican has landed himself upon the shore and whistled a daydreamer's tune. He enjoys the quiet before the Thrushes wake and sing him into a foul mood, one that shares the same putrid quality of fermented fish.

Howard stretches his legs at a casual pace across the shore, hands idling in his pockets, feet kicking some abject stone, mind ruminating along Canterbury thoughts. The morning air is lush with the warming sun, and the cool sea breeze that nips along the nape of Howard's neck is tempered by the sun to a sweet spring morning. It is a perfect morning for tending his bees. He anticipates a large reward of honey to be scraped from the racks of his beehives.

The hum of his bees grows in his ears the closer he gets, but another sound comes mightily overhead, penetrating his thoughts. His daydream is interrupted by a soft choir rising in the air.

Mother,
Oh, Mother—
How the winds change for you,
How the Sun labors for you,
Oh, how the seasons clothe you…

"Why must they always—"

Mother,
Oh, Mother—

"Those kooks are up already!" he grunts to himself.

Their songs, like a faithful pendulum that chimes religiously, bang in his ears as if the pendulum swings pell-mell, hitting the sides of the housed clock. It's not that the Thrushes sing horribly, nor is it the muse of their songs that troubles him.

These land dwellers, he thought, *they just can't give up their mysticism. They just have to worship something.*

"Your mother's a whore!" he yells with a fit.

He will not be tending the bees today.

Howard's "land dwellers," while they don't know the earth as a "biosphere," they will boast a claim that their relationship to the earth is of a more personable one—like a child with its mother. Raw, tender, a rousing love between these Dasein and their "Mother." For them, the trees have become pillars and the vast lazuli dome above, a great temple ceiling; and just listen, all the many voices and sounds reverberating throughout and into the cosmos: the fluting songbirds, the bleating nanny goats, the howling wolves, the chiming crickets, the séancing Dasein, the curling heat of the sun: The Divine talking to itself. The ascetic monk who once beseeched humanity to halt before the grass-hopper may finally take his ease for the crude, everyday-Dasein is now part of a great effort to move gently down the stream of organisms screaming, divine. For Howard, the earth is as simple as it is complex: a thing full of cycles and systems. There is nothing about it that deserves a debt of religion the land dwellers still paid with interest. Howard would rather have these land dwellers go down to the River Lethe, and drink and wash all their mythologies and religion away. However, when he sees them simply as another species of Dasein, he can ignore their self-elected pagandom, for they too seek to "jive the earth on," he would say.

Howard turns around and walks back to his circular observation station like a Dasein with the final word on a matter. And he does have the final word on the matter. As Dublican, he possessed the authority to send any Dasein to the Dead Lands. As long as he could document ecological justification, the final decision would be his.

Anna is startled by the Dublican's shouting. She quickly pulls her paintbrush away from the cave wall and fastens the containers of paint that her father had made and gifted to her last year. She stuffs them in her bag in a frenzy. Her hands pulse blood from a heart filled to the brim with dread. Dread of the Dead Lands. One look into the cave, and the Dublican surely would condemn her. Her faith is made manifest in there. Images of human faces look back at her. Images of flowers bordering her favorite verse which, she recites to herself when she is afraid. For her, it is a sanctuary from the hegemony of the Free World. At times, it feels lonely in there for her (in between her studies), but being cloistered in a cave is all she sees possible for her art. She always breathes upon her latest study right before leaving her cave. She can see the Dublican walking away from his bees in the distance, and she makes for her home in the other direction.

It is the eve of the vernal equinox, and preparations must be made. Spring is an important time for these land dwellers. Spring brings new life, new hope into the world, growth of every carbon-stitched organism. It is made extra special this year for there are several dasein to be recognized in the coming-of-age ceremony. Anna is to be among them.

The ceremony—Anthízo—is traditionally led by the Matron. It is she who stands in front of a garden path of stones (representing the cold winter months) flanked by the Dasein community dressed in green tunics tied by white sashes and their heads adorned by spiraling crowns of wildflowers. The youths to be esteemed glide toward the Matron by the sound of the Thrushes lauding over them. Once they reach the Matron, they receive a steaming cup of milk thistle tea. The youths breathe in its fragrance while the Matron speaks blessing over them. Afterward, they drink.

The sashes are fastened until the Floralian-like holiday known as Kípos (which the land dwellers established on the summer solstice). Upon that day, the sashes come off, and so do the green tunics of the newly initiated. They are to walk naked among the Dasein, and they are to pull the sash off of their partner of choice. The Dasein in wait could tease and beckon but never touch or grab the naked. It unveils a celebration of the power invested in sex, and this flirting occasion empowers those seemingly vulnerable, naked initiates. It is an exciting time for these virgin-youths—now adults—to copulate and affirm this seasonal change of their lives. The build-up of months-long anticipation turns the village into an orgy of heat and pining.

While the peninsula seeks a festive spirit, Anna is as low as mud. Her father's anxiety might rival her own of the coming celebrations and is the cause of her fleeing from cave to room. She tries to think of happier times. She can't. So, she thinks about her cave. Like the monks during World War II did before her, she feels safe in there. The happiest Anna has ever felt is when she's in her cave, painting. Alone with her thoughts, she's allowed to be herself and relish in her arts how she wishes; but this joy is short-lived. She is reminded of an oppressive world, a discriminating world, each time she leaves to go home. Her beautiful smile can be seen by no one each time she enters the cave, and its upward curl falls supine upon her leaving it.

Her smiles are saved for the budding flower of her thoughts: a beautiful world full of artistic virtue whose shape was made by the God of flesh and spirit. What is more, it isn't the shape of a lion or the form of an eagle in which this God reveals himself, but the form and image of man, and this she takes note of. It is for this reason that Anna's paintbrush has invested many weeks' worth of brushstrokes into the shape of God's likeness.

Anna despises the habits of the female Dasein about the peninsula—most especially Sybil, for she is the communal mother. It is Sybil who has been esteemed as "the Matron" by the Crone of the Peninsula, a sort of right-hand to the mysterious witch of the mountain. Sybil isn't just some convert to the ways of the Goddess; she has become an acolyte after the Crone's own heart: strong-willed, passionate, and self-possessed with a certainty that the earth is a sort of crucible to refine the divine self. Being inhabitants of the Free World and no longer living by survival consciousness, Sybil revels and encourages all to live as their authentic, divine selves. She largely encourages this authenticity to be realized through sex. Anna thinks of Cleo's haughty look that night under the Harvest Moon any time she sees Sybil naked, and Anna distrusts her.

Anna eats her evening meal with her father, most of which they pass in silence. Athos has made her favorite meal of tarragon-seasoned tuna with sautéed onions and olives, but it does not encourage any real conversation between them. She sees the look of frustration on his face and ignores it for as long as he can tolerate her silence.

"Anna, what's wrong?"

"Nothing."

"Anna, come on, talk to me."

"I think I'm just tired," she says as she walks her plate into the kitchen.

"Anna! Talk to me!"

Her father's voice grates through the air while his eyes offend her. She loathes these conversations because she knows he holds things back as much as she does, as if they mean to spare one another their grief. It is always in vain, and it always ends like an insult.

"Fine, you want to talk, let's talk."

Her father stands up from his chair and paces some before he responds.

"Have you thought about the ceremony tomorrow?" he asks.

"Of course I have."

"Well? Are you going to attend?"

"I don't have much choice, do I?" she says, offended.

Athos looks at her with a disapproving glance. Anna gives him a sneering look in return. Athos looks toward the future and hopes that she will make the right decision with her body. Anna silently judges him for the hardship he has bestowed on her. Athos's fear grew daily, and he anticipates a future where Anna only gives herself to the wrong use of her body, and in so doing, ignores the author of the very blueprint of those male and female horizons. Athos's fear allows himself to forget that the sexual slopes of the human body were drafted by the mind of God. Every nerve ending that is excited by another's touch was mapped in accordance with the intelligence of God. Athos knows this conceptually, yet the reality of souls and sex are counted as mutually exclusive. He is nearer to the point of villainizing sex altogether because he can't find a single Dasein worthy of his daughter. The problem is, he only knows Dasein, for the world is now short of men. *How could Anna possibly have a future without this sin of the flesh?* go his thoughts: a sin in which the world knows not.

The peninsula once boasted of twenty monasteries made regal by the contemplative studies and curations of artworks, which relished God in hues of gold and red and all manner of earthly gemstones. Most were abandoned and left to nature's mercies. One is still used. It stands with a priceless view of sea and sky all, but a shout away. It is crowned under the climbing mountain. It looks exalted and ennobling—perhaps the reason it is only used for ceremonial and official matters. The Dasein would think themselves more important than they ought if they could use it anytime. It was repurposed as a political center for the judges when a judgement was being issued. When a festival is being prepared it is *the* place to imbue the spirit of the season. The architecture appears more elder than a jinni's beard. Sybil seeks to make it look as magical as one too.

Sybil, is a spritely beauty: a face of golden milk that she and the sun have managed to romance together; even the valley between her sloping chest has been sun-licked and savored. So, too, her buttocks can be found naked and flexing in the early daylight. Sybil seeks to be a walking example of freedom to her daughter, taking after the naturist delights of skin and sun, and so it is her habit to be found with the afternoon breeze on her nipples.

Sybil is a transplant from Albania. There, she was known as Csilla. She fled from her father-appointed husband with her young daughter, Sarasa, when Csilla was twenty years old. She left Albania to escape a marriage that impoverished her rights so severely, rendering her a voiceless woman reduced to "a body waiting at home to be humped," as she would say. She had heard the rumors of women being able to find refuge on a Greek Peninsula. All it would cost her was rinsing herself of the term "woman" and she could go. It wasn't a costly price for her as "woman" was what men called people that were second-rate, somehow deserving less: less respect, less dignity, less privilege. It was an easy choice for her between "Dasein" and "woman." Vulnerable, angry, and dejected, the Crone would seize a perfect acolyte, anointing her as, "Sybil."

The truth is, Sybil loves "a good hump," as she carelessly phrases it, but only on her terms. It is always in daylight. She feels it wise to exercise her energies right before a festival or ceremony in order to be "in-tune with the Mother." She prefers a bed of soft earth when she is preparing herself. This is so she can center and feel the resident energies above and below her. She is always on top of the stiff Dasein of her choosing.

She secretly despises having to incorporate male Dasein into her practice. She doesn't wish to enslave herself again, but she can't ignore the truth of the phallus: its manifestation provided by the Mother. To be at peace with herself, she mounts all her eager Dasein, and as she dances on them, she looks down upon them with Cupid's smile, taking in the effect she has on them, while they look up at her (perhaps like worshipers of Aphrodite, or so she fancies). This posture puts to death her black-widow thoughts of suffocating her dance partners with the plump of her breasts after their energies soar from her throat. There are only so few male Dasein after all.

The once-upon-a-monastery is nearly ready for tomorrow's coming of age ceremony. Sybil is leading in setting up the altar, where she will stand and orchestrate the rite of passage. Her daughter is beside her, gathering the herbs for tomorrow's drink.

"Sarasa, would you bring me the basin from the storage closet?"

Sarasa looks with green eyes at her half-naked mother.

"Of courth, Mama."

Sarasa goes out of the building that stands walled about in a courtyard and climbs a set of stairs that take her to where the basin is stored. She is just about to return when she notices through one of the arched windows a vision of her mother, and there, she stops to watch her. She is speaking with Hera, one of the other initiates in waiting. She can't hear what they speak about or why Hera is smiling so proudly, but hearing their conversation wouldn't have improved Sarasa's mind.

Hera has a beautiful laugh, and it makes Sarasa all the more self-conscious. Sure, Sarasa has taken on her mother's beautiful curtain of blonde, but it doesn't fall on her shoulders like it does on Sybil's. Hers curls and cleaves to her scalp. Sybil's voice seems to melt out of her mouth, a perfect enchantress and the kind of Dasein Sarasa pines to be. She can never evoke an impression beyond darling and adorable with the lisp she speaks with. Her voice is taut from all of the running to and away from tripping over consonants. She learns to even become envious of the bosom she nursed by. Her mother boasts a chest of Cupid's own dreams while she bares a chest only a mouth could cup, and she wants more than sunlight on her body, more than hands, more than eyes. She wants to possess, to be worshipped.

Sarasa returns with the basin and places it behind the altar, but before she lets go of it, her mother asks for her to go fill it up with water for the milk thistle tea that is to be brewed.

"Yeth, Mama" is all she says, a unique address only she makes to Sybil. The courtesy title for the Matron is 'Mother,' and everyone is expected to address Sybil as such. Sarasa makes sure to deviate slightly from the custom in order to subtly remind the Matron that she was first *her* mother. But the role and status of Matron gradually pulls the two away from what intimacy they shared. Sarasa fears she is losing the only family she has, and she fears she won't be wanted by any of the Dasein when the time comes for her to stand naked and vulnerable before her world.

ANTANIA

She came from the dark and into darkness she went. She beds in a dark den, under a dark canopy of trees along Mount Athos when she tires, but she is seldom seen under the "day star," as she calls it. The last time anybody of Biome 1 saw her was the election of the Matron almost a year ago. The Matron says that the Crone is waiting for someone; the right Dasein to be elected into their commune of three. "The triple goddess cannot be complete with just anyone," she says. For months now she has lived off of the flesh of a brown bear that was found wounded. She finished its life and parceled the meat over the winter season. This unknown bit of fortune gives her title more dread and myth than it deserves, but of morals she is always wanting. But these are the days of the Dasein: ethics are ciphered biologically. And Antania—a self-proclaimed goddess—what code of ethics belongs to a crone?

It was just last year when the judges of Biome 1 arrived at a friction in their duties. Sybil was with child, and this new life would need to be reported to the Dublican. They had already tolled the census of Biome 1, and the Dasein numbers were already maxed. The child would need to go. The judges sent word to the crone and an arrangement was made. The night of the child's birth, the crone came down from the mountain in order to help deliver. She left Sybil's home with the child cradled in her arms before a name could be bestowed upon it, like a night bird with its prey. She returned to the mountain. Hours later, the child's cries no longer traveled over the peninsula. No one knows what she did with the child. The two of them just slipped away into that full-moon night. She never speaks of it, not even to Sybil. If asked if she is some kind of evil she will say, "Dark, yes, but not evil."

One of the most tragic things about Antania is her great beauty. Hers is a Gothic castle kind of beauty: a captivating vision, but one you would rather see from afar and keep from her cobwebs. Intricate craftsmanship can be found on her freckled cheek bones, which slope downward to full lips that any lover would adore. Although the map of her face tells of many years traveled, she's maintained a firm grasp on her beauty along the way. The sun has little effect upon one who lives by night. Her eyes ... oh, her eyes—don't look into them for long. One may find themselves tricked into a spell. They were probably a brilliant shade of blue at one point, now turned a sort of steelish gray from all her night gazing. They stare from under a dark mane of hair that could have belonged to a Spaniard, but the bones behind her pale face betray her Slavic heritage.

Look at her there, standing outside of the mouth of her den. She silhouettes against the glowing dusk. She wears a wild dress or robe of some kind, tufts of bear fur jutting from her shoulders, and an earthly crown sits atop of her protesting the heavens. She remains standing, staring, looking toward the silvery glint of failing light. While the Dasein below move into their homes like hurried birds, she stands there as a haunting owl, staring with those eyes. She could be thinking about some other bygone time, romancing it, perhaps a lover, perhaps some other life she left long ago. She could be thinking murderous thoughts too. Thoughts of how to snatch up more children. But no one else stands beside her to pry behind those eyes and into her thoughts, for she secludes herself. Instead, she stands, waiting for the night.

It was over nine thousand moons ago that Antania traded one darkness for another. It was about the same time that she would also trade one name for another.

The "Eco-Revs" that took place before the war stirred the globe into a zeitgeist of maddening stupor. Antania was in Budapest when these started to take place; she went by Theron in those days of borders and nations. She couldn't have been more than twenty-two and was learning what secrets Hungary's Black Metal scene would whisper, screech, yell, and chant in underground clubs. The Ecological Revolutions spread like GMOs across the planet, giving rise to outright desecration of national treasures, artifacts, and relics of the empires. People were feverish. Revolutionaries were deposing of the human race and its ancestry while Theron deposed of her own. A local runaway girl turned midnight muse. She found value in the waning moons just above her thighs and purpose in the galloping lyrics that paced straight for hell. She obliged a band who enjoyed her polyamorous convictions, and they became companions. This went on for almost a year. She would learn dark and esoteric things. Ideas from the Book of Thoth, of sigils, and of Lilith would flirt in her thoughts. Hellish things, even Hell itself didn't seem bad to her. She did, however, quietly dethrone its dark lord. Everything else could be dethroned! Why not? She would ignore the band's chief obsession with Satan and chaos as best she could. Those things seemed foolish to her, like sticking her hand in the fire and watching it cook kind of foolish. She even spoke it out loud once on a night after the concert and crowds dissipated. The lyrics were darker than usual in some of their new songs. Phrases like, "Zombie Jesus semen oozing from your mouths," and "Whoredom or the Abyss." She watched them on their stage that night look as though their fresh blasphemies could be plucked out of the electric air. The darkness was especially palpable, and for reasons unknown she felt inches from grave dirt.

Later that night, and before Theron would give her body away to the most sober member, she challenged the band's ego by assailing against their performance. Theron directed her challenge to Sven, the self-named leader of the band. "What's stopping you all from killing yourselves? That show was a hack job." They laughed at her.

"No, really, what's stopping you?" she demanded. Her voice resounded in the silence. It's not that she grew a conscience or felt the molten heat of conviction. She was just in their frigid shadow far too long and felt its cold for the first time that night. She knew that she needed a new scene, but their cold stares—how deathly still—scared her of their possibility. She knew that she must hold their newfound doubts away from the wild flame of their reason where she hoped her treasonous thoughts could be forgotten. She grew a grin on her face and chuckled, "I'm messing with you fuckers."

But they did not forget. It wasn't but a week later that a band member decided to lure her where a séance was to happen (their typical method of warm-up before a show), but it was all pretense. Theron was thrown to the floor and held down by the throat while the other members put lustful eyes and hands all over her. They howled and laughed as they did it. "Whoredom *and* the Abyss for you," Sven said, crooning in her ear.

When she woke up at the hospital she asked for a pill; anything that would inhibit the growth of an elastic, carbonic fetus—for there was more than one possibility of such growth. When she was released from care she wandered out of Budapest, out of Hungary entirely. By train, bus, or thumb she found the means to flee from Sven's shadow. She went south toward Romania at first, then to Bulgaria. There she learned of her love of mountains. The tree-spired wilds of Bulgaria spoke to a part of her she didn't know existed. It was there that she seemed to shed the coarse skins she wore in Budapest while surviving in a black metal group. She would allow her juvenile knowledge of witchcraft to grow under the hospitality of an old Bulgarian witch who took pity on her. The old witch couldn't have children of her own, and while beyond her fertile years, she felt a mother's heart toward the young woman she'd found wandering along a lonely mountain road. The road meandered by twists and turns where the prehistoric glacier paths did not scar the earth. It was a road where she could chance to meet wolves before she met another person. Theron surely would have given to hypothermia had she not been told to get into a car that puttered up the mountainside. "Child, get in!" demanded the old woman with a voice that could fend off a bear. And without much convincing, Theron got into the old woman's rusted four-door Renault that proved to be as hardy as she. The old woman looked plain and ordinary except that her presence up in the mountains, and without the aid of a man—young or old—was itself, extraordinary. There was much in those mountains to give anyone alarm to how vulnerable they are, especially when alone. The savage cats and wolves that drew nearby and stalked opportune prey; the rough and jagged earth without domesticated land plots for raising food stuffs; the nerve-damaging cold that would numb to the bone; or the occasional traveler with an unknown and questionable integrity. Above all the dangers, even there in the wilderness also, is the man who becomes self-aware of his natural-born strength when beside a lesser power: the man who dreams of omnipotence. The old woman decided to instruct Theron in the ways of mountain life and how to avoid living a wholly dispossessed existence, but not before she saw a tattoo on Theron's body of a familiar symbol, a sigil she had once drawn with finger and ash. She had known its pattern long ago and realized that she didn't pick up a wandering fool along the road but perhaps an angry young woman with a cast iron will. She wondered at the girl's lone trek to nowhere. Was it madness or stubbornness that drove her? The old woman stared long and pondered upon *what* instead of *who* might be the master of her will. "Child, are you crazy, or something?" Theron gave a slow turn of her head. Theron's pale face was turned red, her lips chapped, and small grainy crystals that collected at the corners of her eyes where tears once gushed all communicated together for help. She was without a coat or gloves or hat, not even the coverings on her feet were proper for a walk in the wilderness, much less up a mountainside. She looked pitiful, and even though the old woman didn't know whether she could be trusted, she gave the girl pity—but she knew that even great predators could be made pathetic by the earth's indifference. But, once their strength returned, who knows what a wolf made new would do. "Well? Are you lost?" The old woman's voice was soft, but only as a painted brick: smooth with feminine virtue but blunted and bold like so many lonely cold winters. There was no response. Instead, she saw Theron's lips quivering from the cold that held fast to her, and immediately drove on to get her warm.

The old woman grabbed at Theron's hands and breathed on them, for the frigid mountain air made them stiff. Theron was curled under a great hide of fur; soft long brown hair draped as a blanket around her body. She lay upon a bed with the old woman holding Theron's hands. She would let the warmth inside her hands pulse beside Theron's before she let her near the blaze that cooked in the fireplace. The smell of seasoned pines lifted in the thawing air that dwelt inside a lonely cabin. It was the smell of Theron's salvation. Thoughts of freedom, of sanctuary, of assured repose teemed with those burning pines like incense. Theron never imagined kindness as real, as anything before or beyond the 'please' and 'thank you' sounding from cavalier mouths. She would be forever grateful to the old witch that called herself Zaza. When morning came, Theron heard the clanking of a bowl, slow and repetitive, but dull and hollow: wood against clay. Her eyes met her caregiver's proud gaze and a face writ with benevolence. "Ah, there she is," said Zaza with a peal of joy interrupting the early morning's calm. "Please, do sit down here." She pointed to a chair in front of her. "I'm mixing together some herbs for a cup of tea. Would you like one?"

"Yes," was all Theron said. She felt exceedingly vulnerable and needy but was not ready to be tamed by Zaza's hospitality. A fire was sparked. The water simmered. The herbs steeped. It wasn't until the first sip of tea that Zaza started a conversation with her poor wretch of lost and found. "So, with whom am I drinking tea?" asked Zaza.

"My name is Theron."

"Theron …" the witch's voice disappeared as if into a bygone memory. "No, I can't say that I've met any Theron before, much less anyone so bold as to go marching into a mountainside with nothing but the clothes on their back. And, child, you've got little clothing on your back!"

She leaned back into her chair and waited patiently for a reply, hoping Theron would take the bait. "The tea is good," returned Theron. "What kind?"

"It isn't any *kind*, child. It is a blend of herbs that grow wild out there from where you came from. Now, enough of the dodge. Tell me, what's the story behind your long walk to Zaza's house?"

"I'm not a child. Stop calling me that!" demanded Theron. Her body went rigid, and her eyes were piercing over the mug of tea like a vindictive siren glaring from outside her murky waters.

"Theron, you forget whose house you're making demands in." Zaza may have been well along in years, but they didn't make her frail in spirit. Her eyes beamed back with rebuke by the authority of the wrinkles that framed them. The both of them stared for a moment until Theron ricocheted Zaza's stern look. She stood up with haste and was making her way to the door before her departure was protested. "Where are you going? Hold on a minute. Theron, stop!" Zaza barred Theron's escape with a firm stance in front of the door. She looked like a mountain lion—calm yet ready to pounce: her stance was wide while her hands still clasped the mug of fresh tea. Theron was at once beside herself from the spritely old woman yet made irritable from the impasse she presented, and it was in that moment that she could no longer run aimlessly from Sven's shadow. She would be made to confront her travels and reasons, but the hesitation under her tongue was a savor that she could not ignore; she was not yet ready. At once and without warning, Zaza uttered a combination of sounds that were unfamiliar to Theron. They were sharp and choppy and subtle and Slavic. Theron's face flexed with fright as the sounds became words, and words turned to phrases that hailed a thick barrage against her. Zaza's voice grew louder, and her eyes did not blink while her tongue dribbled in her mouth an undiscernible spell. Theron's pulse quickened, her hands grew weak, and she shifted from side to side. She let the mug crash to the floor in front of her and returned a horrified look to the droning Zaza. Theron didn't know if her body was made weak by the tea she drank or by the spell she opined was being ushered from the old woman. She thought that perhaps she was poisoned as the room became a blur while her knees were buckling. Theron fell to the floor with the likeness of a marionette doll and the puppeteer quickly advanced upon her.

Thereon was in and out of consciousness, for it was being robbed of her—it was not entirely hers to will. She was abducted into a trance state in order for the old witch to learn her secrets. In between twitches and trembles, Theron spoke. She spoke of Sven, of the band, of the fear, of things she never told a soul: the searing memory of refused kinship. Out there, somewhere along the concrete wilds of Budapest was a woman with a like-countenance and a man whose lips never spoke her name. Given a bastard's inheritance, it was only a matter of time till Theron would become a vagrant herself. The vagrant Zaza beheld lay there under toiling brow, and a panting fit was soon upon her. Zaza stooped low in order to whisper into Theron's ear the sweet words of her release, and instantly, Theron rose up from the floor. She looked all around her to find herself in the midst of a circle of salts powdered neatly, ceremoniously. She could not yet see it herself, but she wore a painted sigil across her forehead and below it, eyes wide with fear. Theron backed away from Zaza until she ran into a wall. "What did you do to me?" asked Theron. "Was I dreaming or—"

"You were confessing," said Zaza. "I now know all of your darkest secrets. There's no use in hiding the truth from me any longer."

Theron gave her a puzzled look. "You don't believe me, do you? I know why it is you are running away, or from whom, rather. I know of Budapest, the reason for your hospital visit, I even know of the sigil that you have tattooed on your body, but what I don't know is why, of all the sigils, you chose *revenge*."

"Because ... screw them!"

"Who?"

"Men. All of them: boyfriends, husbands, fathers; all of them deserve, either by a little or by a lot, a revenge ending."

"Listen, if it's revenge you want, you will need to do it smarter than this aimless wandering of yours. True revenge is taking away your need of them."

"But I don't need them!"

"Then why is there pain in your response? Pain is often masked by anger. You may fool the young, you may even fool yourself with that anger, but you cannot fool an old girl like me."

Theron went silent.

Theron was quiet for the rest of the day and lived in that place between resentment and fear. She felt resentment toward Zaza because her keen wit seemed to allow her into the privacy of Theron's vengeful heart. Then there was the fear of being incapable of protecting herself, the fear of indebting herself once again to a male companion, and the fear of abuse. She went quiet for hours, and this troubled Zaza at first until she came up with a solution, which she announced over dinner.

"I've got it! You require a new name. A name that is bold, but a name that gives you the freedom to self-determine your qualities. All of your life has been a tragedy. In your past they called you Theron; but in your future, they shall call you Antania."

No later than when twilight shadows fell did Zaza prophesy over Theron, and no sooner than when the moon rose did Theron decide her future self to be realized.

Antania had welcomed the first day of her new self with more awe and satisfaction than she knew to be possible. She felt like someone who was given the cure to her cancer. Zaza had diagnosed the cancer as "Theron" and provided a new identity with varied possibilities as cure. Such a simple solution, and with only three syllables, Zaza was able to curb the impetuous fits of fear. Antania started the morning by addressing herself in the mirror as such: "Hello, my name is, Antania." She stared long and steady into the oval mirror that hung over a dresser and water basin. For the first time in her wandering, a grin washed over her face; for in that moment she felt freer than she had ever been, more free and less free radical. It was a grin of pure gold. Antania would eventually share her smile with her host as she warmed up to the old woman like a child with their grandmother. Instead of stories and sweets, Zaza gave her knowledge of many things. Zaza seemed to Antania as an alchemic priestess with her great repertoire of hidden knowledge, things she could bore out of the earth right in front of Antania and with the right mixture behold a tonic, a poison, a salve. Antania would learn to utter new chants, she would add to her knowledge the history of great mages, and the names of resident spirits to which Zaza looked for aid. Antania often marveled at how this old woman could live alone, but when she saw how Zaza's face looked after beseeching the spirits, she realized her secret. Zaza wasn't truly alone.

"How do you know what spirits to call to?" asked Antania. The two were pruning a shrub of its leaves as part of their daily forage. Zaza leaned back while staring. She seemed surprised by the question.

"Well, you ask it its name first," she said coyly. They laughed together, but it was a short-lived sound in Antania's mouth. Her face went placid while her thoughts idled in memory. "What is it?" asked Zaza.

"I've always been alone. When I met you up here in the mountains, with no one else, I thought of how you would understand me; that you would know what it's like to be alone. But I've seen you talking with spirits. Turns out, you aren't alone after all. I have envied you since, and I don't know how to shake this feeling."

"It is true, Theron was alone, but Antania is not," said Zaza almost sternly. She placed her hand on Antania's shoulder and gave it a squeeze. Antania wanted to cry, but she didn't want the old woman to know just how much she clung to those words; she held enough power over her as it was, and she didn't wish to give her more. But a little time turns all history into irony: Antania would cry, she would fear overwhelming power, and she would feel alone once more when the autumn came. The old witch hadn't learned how to live forever, nor did she have any talent for resurrection. News didn't reach up in those mountains. Therefore, when the bands of rebels came, they came as a lightning-born firewall that only knows to climb mountains and leave scourging paths of ruin. The revolutionaries came to cull humanity from wherever and whatever evidenced them in places the Eco Revs deemed sacred. Antania would have strength enough to flee her pursuers. Zaza would decide a last stand: as a lioness of the mountain she stood; as a bludgeoned old woman, she fell. Zaza had taught Antania that a different way to live is possible, even for her; but revolution can displace the best of intentions.

In the months to come, Antania would eat by the sweat of her thighs and many a man reached for her body with worshipping hands as if communing under some nocturne goddess. A goddess who stole her sacrificial offerings when slumber took them. Unlike Theron, Antania never sought to remain in the company of men beyond the night. It was only ever a bartering act, and she became quite skilled at it. She was a desperate woman in desperate times.

The Revolution always brought its revolutionaries near. Romanian castles crumbled before them and from the rubble they shouted like conquerors. When Bulgarian churches were being blown apart like bursting whale flesh, she felt dread. Not because she feared for the orthodox and the religious, but because she knew what people who gave into chaos are capable of, and she would leave Bulgaria for Northern Greece by her naked thumbs.

Several years later, she arrived at Biome 1, not long after the Dasein takeover. Once a haunt of men and orthodoxy, now a wildland that resides somewhere between fable and science-fiction. Some Arcadian like state hovered over the peninsula where a bucolic varnish could be found to tease the mind with ideas like, "should be," and "if only" had now materialized. Antania saw it as a lush resort where Nature's virtues and Humanity's natures could thrive, and so could she.

One day she hiked across the peninsula to gather whatever she could carry that might be of use to her. She wandered into an abandoned monastery once called Xenophontos. It was the closest thing to a castle she'd walked through. Its great arched walkways, a mosaic of flagstone roads surrounding and paths throughout, the vast walls that stood the monastery up onto a tilt of the head made it feel like a fortress. The dark hallways seemed to be full of nothing but the sound of her footsteps. It smelled like neglected earthenware, and she inhaled the stale-bread air with a grin. It grew large when she saw before her a wine cellar, still stocked. It was locally bottled and now a couple of decades old. Antania grabbed several bottles and clanked them into a stitched leather bag she carried for whatever goods she would find. She found an old corkscrew, and she used it to open one of the bottles. The cork squealed out of the bottle neck, and she held the brim to her nose. The robust aroma of the Athonite wine smelled like a thousand hues of scarlet that deserved a sommelier's nose rather than hers. It seemed to deserve some other mouth too. She drank it straight from the bottle without any ceremony while surrounded by all the ritual and tradition of thousands of years. She pursed her lips around the bottle and let the work of the Patriarchy fall over her tongue and into her stomach. She turned and walked out, sipping on her bottle.

She wandered some more, looking at the artistic embellishments of the old orthodox stronghold. It was mostly architectural decisions not so easily taken. There were no more religious pictures hanging on the walls. No more golden crosses. Not even the spiraling chandeliers remained. Her browsing led to a dark room of stone and mortar and wooden shelves. When she drew closer to the woodwork, she realized that the room was used as a catacomb. The shelves bore hundreds of skulls, lined and stacked with intent, which she thought humorous and belted out a laugh for they were the skulls of monks. Centuries of monk-lives were ranked and filed before Antania, and to her was the victory. She was the last one standing.

"Oh, this is precious. And just look at yourselves now." She put her bottle down in order to get a better look. She reached toward the cobwebbed skulls and laughed some more. When she plucked one of the heads from the shelf, she noticed that the bottom jawbone was no longer attached. When she saw this, she made a buck-toothed smile back at the skull. "So handsome." She pulled the skull in and kissed in front of it where a mouth once was. She laughed again, only this time, louder than before. A weathered inscription was painted across the two spheres of the frontal cranial bone, but its aging and dust dimmed the lettering. She picked up her bottle and carried the skull out of the room with the hopes of gaining a better look at the words. The light only showed that it was Greek, but still indiscernible. And she, with a newfound liquored mood, took the skull with both hands and dragged her tongue across it so that the words may be clearer. The message in its entirety could not be made out, but what she did recognize read as δόξα της ανθρωπότητας. This made her giggle with delight. She picked up the bottle once again and took in a mouthful of the aged wine and then spit it all over the skull till it was dripping in a faint red highlight. Once she took in another gulp of the wine, she palmed the skull into her leather bag and continued her treasure hunt through the senile structure that once was invigorated by the prayers of living men.

INVASIVE SPECIES

Anna and her father continue their conversation late into the night. It meanders between fear and anger and into tidbits of her father's curious knowledge. He decides to cool his tongue from probing further into Anna's intentions for the ceremony and begins a slow and steady roundabout turn upon her daily habit for early morning outings instead.

"It's because culture imitates Art far more than Art imitates culture that artists are to be weary," says Athos. He speaks with grave authority, as if he thought of this aphorism himself. Anna tries to not look so impressed or shaken by his words. They sit at the kitchen table, she with her chin in her palm. "Leaders," he continues, "are weary of artists because they know this. A governor would much rather kill an artist than kill a whole city for its adoption of the provocative ideas founded in the art of an artist. It's more ecological that way," he says with a sideways smirk, for he'd borrowed a Dasein term to make his point. Anna rolls her eyes.

'More ecological' is a common saying that has replaced the traditional value system of money. There is no more "It's more economical" way of thinking. Instead, wisdom is to be found in decisions with positive impacts upon the biome.

Athos is about to proceed further when Anna becomes impatient with him.

"Why are you telling me all of this?" asks Anna.

Athos looks at her, sending his brows forward on his face, but he pauses to calculate his response. He is preparing a teaching moment, like his father did with him, and so the son of an Art History Professor proceeding, "I suppose you haven't heard of the *Madonna del Parto?*"

"Who?" asks Anna.

"It was a profound fresco painted by Piero Della Francesca, 1400s, and the image consisted of Mary the mother of God, who was pregnant, garbed in blue, and shown with a vertical gash across her belly. The gash shined white as snow, suggesting that the glory of Heaven was vested within Mary. Two angels stood beside her lifting pomegranate curtains away from her like servants beside royalty. For the believer, it was a significant scene—she was practically speaking the ark of the new covenant between God and mankind. It was an image of the promise of Heaven on earth."

"Okay, Papa, get to the point," says Anna, slowly drumming her fingers on her cheek.

"Well, my point is ... that painting bore great theological content. Content that not only portrayed the reflections of an artist musing about his God, but content that incited the viewer into acknowledging God's own grace. The world was made descendant of an old promise under the subject matter of the *Madonna del Parto*, but the world rejected both the promise and God. It was only a matter of time that the fresco would be rejected likewise. For a while, unbelievers would tolerate the painting and embrace what they liked about it: the pomegranates, which latticed the rich curtains, or the lapis lazuli of Mary's dress taken from the bosom of what used to be Afghanistan. But as the Free

World decided tolerance was too kind. The fresco was destroyed over two decades ago now, just before you were born."

Anna is restless inside. She knows what her father is trying to get at, but she doesn't like it. She feels stifled by the world, as if cornered into a cave—a world that she doesn't wish harm to but that would cause great harm to her because it finds her paintings disagreeable. Instead of talking about this frustration, she allows it to ferment in the pit of her, and her father receives Anna's disdain for the world instead.

"Why can't you just speak plainly about things?" she says despairingly. "You always have to ramble on before saying what you mean. Just say what you mean!"

"All right then, where were you this morning?" he asks.

"What? What does that have to do with your, Mr. Francesca?"

"Look there," he says, pointing at her green cloak hanging off a neighboring chair. "There is paint on the hem of your cloak. You've been painting again."

"And so what if I have? How is it that you teach me about the arts and encourage me in it, even made me paint just last year, and now here you are scolding me about *painting!*" Anna speaks furiously. Her hands raise and fingers splay out from each other.

Athos tries to get past the awkward stalemate.

"Art is not what you see, but what you make others see," — more from some forgotten authority on the matter.

"Papa, I know!"

"Well … then you know how dangerous it is to leave our home to go paint what you wish."

"Oh, and it's so much safer in the house!" she exclaims, waving at the surrounding glass structure.

Perhaps Athos is checkmated after all, but a father's love … "Anna, my darling—"

"Don't," she demands, her anger so welled up inside she can't do anything but stand up. She is getting ready to leave the room when her father steps toward her and embraces her.

"Anna, I love you. I care for you. You will always be my penguin, and I just want to protect you. That's what a father is supposed to do."

Anna begins to cry. Her thoughts turn to the ceremony that is now less than twelve hours away. She wants her father to do what he said he's supposed to do, to protect her. The Kípos festival isn't for another couple of months, when she will be expected to participate in public what she thinks is a very private matter. Anthízo is more than just acknowledging her coming of age but as advertisement that Anna will now be a participant in this year's celebration of Kípos, and to refuse them both; well that was just it, no one ever refused.

"I don't think I can go through with the ceremony tomorrow. Papa, please. Don't let them make me." Anna's lip quivers. She leans her forehead into Athos's shoulder and listens to the resounding silence. All of her thoughts ignore the possibility of her as an invasive species to be cut off from the biome, and instead she dwells on Anthízo and Kípos. What the Dasein count as freedom, Anna considers as slavery. Put out or get out is the slogan she imagines.

Athos is eating his own words: *to protect you ... that's what a father is supposed to do.* He is the only real father here on the peninsula. All the other male Dasein seek the next "blessed" opportunity to cascade their bodies over another Dasein. Athos feels the weight of Anna's life on his shoulders while all the other male Dasein only feel the weight of saliva on their tongues. The Free World does not promote things like monogamy, hetero-sexual companionship. Marriage has even been made a curious word and no longer in the greater vocabulary of Dasein-kind. Fathers? Only mama birds; the male Dasein are no more useful than roosters strutting about. Whenever Athos said, "A father is supposed to ..." it has to be true for he is *the* father she had available. "Only *men* can be fathers," he'd once said to Anna when she wondered about the other male Dasein on the peninsula. "Those fellas out there only want ..." he paused to think of different words. "Well, you know what they want, don't you? No need in saying it out loud."

"My vagina," said Anna. A word she had to learn from Cleo. Athos's teeth smashed together and so did his face when he heard the word. It wasn't that he was a prude; he had known its magic, felt its heat, known its kiss. But, to think that his daughter would be known in the same way, perhaps in some pagan way, tormented him more than any tusked elephant in the room could.

"Yes," he'd said cringingly. He continued his thought: "Only men can be fathers, but men don't exist anymore. They wanted to be something less, something more animal than human." His own thought of men-turned-animal scared him. He was scared for his daughter. *What would come of her?* He did not prepare for this.

"So then why didn't you do the same? Become like the others?"

He did, however, look forward to this question all her life. Even though they were in their home, Athos looked up and around to see if anyone or anything were watching them. Nothing. He leaned closer to Anna with a face no longer menaced by vaginas. "I couldn't. God wouldn't let me do such a thing to his reputation."

"Reputation? What are you talking about?"

"You see I am *a* father, but I am not *the* Father. When men still existed in the world, some took the chance to become a father knowing that they would be sharing the title "father" with God the Father. Those who sought to share that relationship did so in order to help their children understand the heart of God, his father's heart. Of course, not many did that well. I sometimes wonder how well I'm doing with you."

He'd had the words then, but now, all he can think of us guilt, and whose fault it is that Anna will have to face such things.

What a father is supposed to do ... What is a father supposed to do now?

Athos slips out of the house in order to walk with his restless thoughts. The day is turning the page to night. Athos hopes the night will be a long one, or at least long enough for a miracle to happen. They don't usually happen overnight—even Jesus took about nine months.

He walks beside the sea where his thoughts leave the peninsula, the present, and drift to a time before he feared for Anna. He was just a man, and she was just a woman—that's what he told himself then. "What have I done," he whispers.

It was late one night when he met "just a woman" at a music festival. Somehow, the festival still managed to stage the expected performing artists while the world was plagued by revolution and strife. He had always excused his behavior that night by his being disarmed by alcohol. One sin was better than the other, yet he'd never suggest such a thing out loud. One sin would become another.

He saw her dancing on the rooftop of a hotel he was staying at while taking holiday. She beckoned him to dance, with her chicly dressed body and a voluptuous Bellucci smile. Below her naked shoulders hung a black see-through halter-neck blouse hemmed in lace. Below the lace she wore a ruffled bohemian skirt, and under her skirt, naked feet danced. It took a Samson-like effort to ignore his desire to admire the gentle slopes of her breasts, marble against the dark blouse. They were trying to peek out and see their new admirer. He couldn't tell if the blood in his face was from the drinks or from his just-a-man imagination. He walked toward her.

"There's nothing more dangerous in the world than a woman who knows she's beautiful," he'd said. Even in his drunken state he quipped aphorisms. His life was always one aphorism after the other.

"Maybe all *she* knows is how your face looks right now," said the woman. His face slipped a grin, and his once-hazel now-drunken eyes stared at her while she stared back with large blue eyes framed in the blackest mascara she could find. Those eyes cheated logic, and their power was great enough to distract him from the sterling nose ring looped through her septum. She grabbed the back of her neck with both hands and tilted her head slightly as she leaned into the music around her. His lips parted as hers parted. She could see him coming undone. She looked at him now looking at her mouth. Her smile would interrupt his daydreaming. "Thirsty?" she asked. "Come on, follow me." And she grabbed him by the hand, leading him toward the bar like Delilah leading Samson by the beard. Together they zigzagged around the glowing pool and festive crowd. The mood was wilder than it should have been, perhaps the carbon-riddled germ of revolution was airborne. It wasn't enough for there to be festive stringed lights but shooting roman candles also. The scantily clad women weren't naked enough; there had to be skinny dippers in the pool. The current talent on set wasn't jovial enough; there had to be a group of fans howling the lyrics also. "Do you have Pálinka back there?" she asked. The bartender shook his head. She looked back at her victim with pouty lips. He moved in to make a scene about this outrageous fact.

"What do you mean, no Pálinka? he asked. He had never heard of this drink before but spoke in a way that seemed to charm both the woman and the bartender. "Why, this is absurd! Do you expect this woman to guzzle down some rotgut booze instead?"

"So feisty," said the male bartender. "I like that." And with a wink and stare the bartender confused the scene further. The three of them were deadlocked in an awkward pause that seemed to ignore the party about them.

"Um, he's mine thank you very much. Get your own!" said the woman. The bartender pursed his lips at them, and Delilah grabbed her Samson and pulled him away.

"Thanks, I didn't plan for that," he said.

"Come on, let's ditch the party," she said to him with an accent he couldn't yet place.

"Wait, I don't even know your name."

"You need a name?" she asked coyly.

"Babies need a name. I *want* yours."

"Is that all you want?" she asked with a raised brow. He laughed out loud. "Come on. Besides, it's a few kilometers' walk from here." Everything about her tantalized him. The eyes, the vaguely northern accent, her flirty confidence—like that of a street walker—that pulled on him like gravity.

They walked under a pallid sky through a city that was named after a general's wife. An unrecognizable city with only vestiges of its Graeco-Roman glories suffocated by the swell of globalism's storms. People of all cultures thundered on this international hub. Techies brought new industries. Spiritualists further nuanced the great myriad of beliefs. Scientists informed more advanced methods of sustainable development practices. Artists

of all genres came bending the boundaries of cultural appropria-
tions till things like the Roman Arch was deemed antagonistic
and unbecoming of the present. Gray-haired and romantic insti-
tutions challenged such claims but without victory. The faint
shadow of Thessaloniki's past was caught in a twilight where only
a single Roman Arch remained. There was talk of dismantling
it in order to raise a vertical structure that would house thousands of global citizens. Such were the effects upon the citizenry
of Thessaloniki, and this modern specter haunted the man and
woman as they walked.

"My name is Alexander. What's yours?"

"Antania."

"I don't believe I've ever known anyone by that name before. It's
beautiful. I can't place your accent either. Where are you from?"

But Antania wouldn't give up much else about herself. "All over
really," was all she said.

Their hour-long walk would include more back-and-forth flirts.
Eventually, the intoxicated Alexander would learn that he was
being led to a cemetery. "What! A graveyard? This is where you
wanted to go instead?" Alexander was surprised, but his questions
were punctuated by chuckling. He looked at their destination,
and before him stood the Zeitenlik Military Cemetery. Grave-
yards were a thing of the past and no longer sanctioned. Some
were even recycled into something else of more ecological benefit.
This gravesite still remained due to its multi-national significance.
In it bore the bones of more than twenty thousand soldiers. The
very bones of soldiers from World War I. "But it's closed," said
Alexander.

"And?" Antania looked at him with daring eyes.

"Ah, fine. We didn't walk all this way for nothing now, did
we?" They snuck into the memorial park, and when they walked

farther into the dark, they noticed a pale shape contrast the vast shadow they strolled through. It was a cross. Alexander could see more of them issuing before him. It was a darker night than other nights. Such that those crosses could only be seen if he was looking for their shape. Alexander could hear her as she was zigzagging through the graves, as if doing a slalom around all the crosses in her path. Without any notice, she decided the walk was over. She dripped herself down on some soldier's grave and called out to Alexander.

"Come here and fuck me," she commanded.

Alexander was sloshed, but even so, a gnat-size voice buzzed in his thoughts to convict him. The voice of his father—whom he loved dearly—ushered with thoughts of God and his divinely appointed conditions to zest in sexual appetites, all but a gnat-sized shout. The dark with its dusky beauty continued to call out to him. She began to moan his name. This sound excited him and produced a thrill that only lovers should know, and he looked for where her voice sounded. There, in a dark cemetery, beside a pale marble cross and six feet above some dead hero, Anna was created. Alexander would forever feel the weight of Antania's saliva on his tongue. His thoughts return to the peninsula, and he shakes his head, asking out loud again, "What have I done? Lord, what have I done?"

Athos drifts farther along the shore. The beauty of the scene surprises him. The night sky is tethered to a waning moon, and the water shimmers its moon glade serenely. The heavens are not darker than the peninsula but dark enough for Athos to see countless stars salt the sky. Wafts of the sea trick him into thinking he can taste the brine of the night. Thoughts of salty meat on the spit and feasting water his mouth. Thoughts of the festivals to come protrud mightier in his thoughts, and his thoughts ground in fear once again.

Once his eyes fall from the sky, he sees the electric glow of the observation station about three hundred meters in front of him. "Hello there," comes a male's voice from the dark.

"Ah!" is all Athos can speak in return, and the voice laughs at him in response.

"Hello! What … who's there?" asks Athos.

"I be Howard Phillips," says the voice gaily. Athos turns toward the voice and smells the reason for Howard's upstaged announcement. He has been drinking. Then comes a tone of exaggerated bass, "The Dublican …" he says, half-mockingly and yet placating the local's fear of him. Athos hasn't personally met him yet.

"And who might you be?"

"Athos," he says, trying to ignore the terrible authority endowed to Howard.

"How fitting. Whatcha doin', Athos?" Athos can't see Howard's face, only his silhouette, and so it makes for a troubled beginning in conversation. He doesn't know how to take him. Should he converse with him as *Howard* or as *the Dublican*?

"Trying to collect my wits is all."

"Well, here I was thinking the peninsula was loitering wit' notin' but half-wits and goons."

*I'm talking with Howard.*Perhaps it is the drink. Perhaps it is the fact that the dark seems to conceal Howard like a mask that makes him talk casually with one of his subjects of study. Either way, Athos is relaxed enough to actually converse about whatever Howard wants to talk about.

"Say, how old are ya? Aren't ya—"

"Forty-eight," replies Athos.

"Ha! You and me, we're the ol' gooses of this here whoredom. It's as if pages of *Fanny Hill* have been torn out and strewn across the peninsula, if ya know what I mean."

Athos laughs at his poignant but backhanded remark. "What's that woman's name who's always strutt'n about naked?" Howard asks without any hesitation of using the word *woman*, but the pause Athos gives, gives Howard time to see his wrong word usage. "Old habits I suppose. Ya know what I mean." And just like that, Howard excuses himself from the new world decorum. Howard can't see it, but Athos is smiling like he once did when he had a friend. Before his habitation on Biome 1. Before Man became Dasein.

"Sybil," laughs Athos.

"That ol' girl doesn't give a damn. Stretch marks and all, she trots around like she's Eve herself." It is curious to Athos that such an authority of Science would repeat Eve's name when she belongs to what is counted as farce. Still more curious to Athos is the fact that Howard has observed Sybil enough to notice her stretch marks. *Just how close does Howard observe the Dasein with his drones?* Athos wonders. He wonders what else Howard will say.

"Would you care for a drink?" asks Howard.

"What is it?"

"This ain't any ol' loopy juice. This is my own batch of mead." Athos hasn't had mead in probably decades.

"Isn't that stuff illegal now?"

"Do you want some or not? Besides, you're drinking with," he switches to the low mocking tone, "the Dublican," and laughs some more.

"Well then, don't mind if I do." Athos takes the flask-like container saying, "Yamas!" and drinks. "Oh, that's good!"

"Bet your ass it is." The two of them let the mead warm the hollow left inside of them, and for the first time in years they both feel like men again, as if drinking with a friend, and Howard begins to talk as if they are.

"Ya remember what the world was like before all this, right?" asks Howard.

"I do."

The two stare off into the vast night sky and let the idea germinate into some unknown crop of musings.

"I miss going to the pub. Sitting on a bar stool. Hearing the kegs let loose and feeling the foam sink into my gut until the need to belch comes out uninvited."

"Yes, those were some happy days." Athos agrees, partly in earnest, partly to gauge the conversation further.

"And what about you? What do you miss?"

"Museums," says Athos.

"Museums? Those were always good for a bore—maybe if there's beer ..." Howard laughs at himself and then at Athos for his surprising answer.

"Seriously," Athos continues. "Museums held so much knowledge of cultures, so much art and artifact of the ancients. It's almost like feeling a bit lost without them. Like feeling quarantined without them." Howard senses Athos's sincerity and chooses to gulp down more mead if he is to entertain the conversation any longer.

"I miss the artworks one could find in a museum. So many perspectives, and so many ideas presented. They were like essays of intellectuals, but in a different form. Each had a thesis; some you couldn't ignore but had to contend with them. All striving towards truth and virtuosity—"

"Hold on!" says Howard with careless intent to cut him off. "Stop right there before you wander back into the dissociative identities of our past." Howard is impatient with anyone who romances the ideologies of the old world and can sense its suffixed thought to Athos's dreaming of museums. Instead of tolerating it further, Howard cuts to the chase on the matter and set to reappropriate Athos's mind.

"Listen, Pluralism … in a global state, it was never going to work. It just wasn't sustainable. I mean really, how did anyone think that we could live in a world where every truth is equal? More than that, a world where peace can be had by followers of say, God? Or Allah? Elohim?" Howard's last remark puts Athos on alert, and he treads lightly in all this friendly talk.

"It's a strange thing to note … the peninsula that is," Athos stutters to point out the present irony. "The world thinkers ridded the earth of religion of every kind but raised the maypole of Naturalism. The people here quite literally dance around that pole."

"Indeed, they do. Oh, how I loathe these people. Them, with all of their nature-loving ritual and magic. Humanity has always had a disadvantage when the first myth broke out."

Athos notices Howard's change in demeanor, the seriousness the conversation takes on, and how he becomes more aware of the words he uses. It seems as though Howard is laboring to articulate upon the world's solution for world peace. Evidently, Howard thinks of these things often. After all, working by oneself affords time to think. The stalling effort Athos notices between bouts of silence may have been an effort to organize his many thoughts on the matter or to wait for his drunk mind to catch up.

"Societies have always been weak at the knees for gods and goddesses, an unfortunate reality," says Howard. The cantering conversation turns to trotting. "We learned from intersectionality that homo sapiens are fragile beings that cannot be given the artificial freedoms they once had. Freedoms found in air travel for instance. Being dropped into another country, another culture, where more than tongues differ. We scientists are now efficiently capable to protect the harmony of every ecosystem, and it was first necessary to limit species drifting into other biomes, to include homo sapiens."

Athos has never heard the reason for their being isolated to a single biome before. "So, what is it exactly that is the problem for people, sorry—Dasein, that they require such isolation?" A flash of fear strikes in his mind; he is forgetting himself and forgetting who he is talking to, and his language proves so.

"First, a word on your terms. The only reason why the word 'Dasein' has become a necessity is because people couldn't help but look backward. And what did they find? All those myths about them, about us, and then perpetuate them to their children. Mankind was a mistake. Dasein is on purpose, and theirs is a more trustworthy future." But upon this last thought, Howard mumbles to himself something, forgetting to state his second claim, and looks up at the night sky. Athos looks to see what Howard sees. The carbon in his thoughts has mulled into something bitter.

"Turns out there are assholes in space too," says Howard.

"What are you talking about?" asks Athos. He can't help laughing.

"Black, hideous assholes, but these holes ingest everything rather than digest." The two men stand under the expanse—one marvels, the other gawks at the billions of stars winking. Athos gives pause before he queries.

"What's bothering you?" he asks, forgetting his own troubles. He still doesn't know the full breadth of Howard's disdain for the Dasein on Biome 1. Howard wants nothing to do with the place. He is here as a promotional steppingstone toward his interest in Space Command, where they are preparing for a future among the stars. He pines for some extraterrestrial day where it is his foot that steps on foreign matter surrounded by foreign stars. His hope is not in the world's triumph of world peace, and hope is hardly in him. Like any other Dasein, he, too, lives in the same subcortical cave in the brain—the amygdala; he, too, fears a great many fears.

"Don't you see? Look around us. Here we are on this blue geomorph trying to perfect the chaos, regulating the variables, ordering the species of every class—of every domain, and in every biome. Meanwhile … there above us," he says, pointing with a crooked finger and a ninety degree turn of his wrist that moves against the stars, "swirling nothingness, pockets of space where all consciousness ceases to exist. Light! Light itself cannot outrun them!" His lips part and pause while his thoughts traverse from one atom to the next in a covalent bond of frenzied musing. Howard is possessed in thought. Athos can see that it is a futile thing to interrupt his streaming consciousness. He lets him proceed with his spinning mind. Trotting thoughts now become a full gallop.

"Light … perfect, incorruptible light … is made a thing to be stolen and forgot in those holes. And we … parasitic, greedy homo sapiens would rather steal life and land and forget all other species like indifferent black holes. Dasein like me are necessary to stymie our own self-destruction, and considering all of our history—which you well know—we have arrived at a sort of perfection that is measured by the greater homeostasis of this planet. And for what? To go sailing along the cosmos into some future disappearing trick!" he snarls. "We've redeemed all the world and its children are counted blessed. Blessed!" he hisses. "Blessed are we the future benefactors of a perforated universe whose indifference you admire there looking up into those stars. You see the glint and brilliance of the sky. I can't help but think of the invisible whirlpool that will surely pull us into one eternal night."

Howard's last thought shivers into Athos's curiosity. The darkness of Howard's thoughts is seen beside the light of Athos's mind. He can't help but think of Caravaggio's use of Tenebrism—extreme darkness beside a rich contrast of light. The two stand beside one another, juxtaposed in the same tenebrous manner as like starlight beside a black hole. The poem of the world seems to be either a comedy or a tragedy—there is no in between. Athos thinks about how the weight of gravity seems to fall heavy upon Caravaggio's work and make a scene feel more ominous than the next painter's brush; about how light is a physical source of hope for all, and how without it one is sure to become victim of hideous crawling thoughts like ghastly Cthulean dreams.

Howard swirls his container, looking sideways into it as he does, and springs it above his head and shouts, "To Zarathustra!" He laughs a hard, guttural laugh after he finishes his mead; he throws the container into the sea and proceeds toward his quarters.

It may well be that Athos is the only one on the peninsula that knows anything about the name in which Howard has just saluted. A name, now centuries old, forgotten. Yet resurrected by a "man of science"? Athos knows of it because of his father. Said that the man behind the name was in large part to blame for encouraging such wretched behaviors; that *his* thoughts were like a consuming fire that changed the world forever. It scares Athos to think that the ideals of a madman have informed Howard. *Truly, no one here is safe with this man. No amount of science can save him.*

"You all right, friend?" Athos calls out. But Howard just waves him off while stumbling to bed. Athos thinks bookending the question with "friend" will percolate in Howard's mind and rapport would bubble between them. Maybe his artisan daughter would be spared a death sentence, but could she live in the purgatory of self-censorship? Could she exile her soul? Exile her God, whom all her art aspires toward? Could she really tolerate a life paced by witchcraft? Athos weeps as he walks back home.

ANTHÍZO

Cool morning light shines on twisting, talon-like fingers that wisp through the air. Those hands stretch out above and around a Dasein of female form dressed in black, her hair long and falling backward toward the grassy earth. She slowly bends her spine back, as if strung by some sadist puppeteer, and is suspended like this for a purpose whispered to her in the dark. It is Antania. She careens into the worshipers' song that sings through the air. She looks like a mad maestro conducting the Thrushes' song about the maidens three. And yet, neither can see the other. The carbon between them includes many fields of trees. Antania is exorcising something out of herself in a wild-kept field while the Thrushes sing joyously, delighting in the day ahead from the balcony of the repurposed monastery.

Anna rises early, before the sun, before the song in the air. She walks up the mountain looking for the flower made special by Father Stephanos. The flower she adores most, the snowdrop. It is the rarest flower on the peninsula, for it blooms early in the year, is only seen at the higher elevations of the mountain, and its lifespan is short. There are other flowers already beginning to bloom now, but she adores the snowdrop most. Sure, the rose is always a beauty worthy to be pricked by, but the snowdrop can grow straight up and through a bed of snow. She can't feel the hope that her faith aspires toward, so she hikes up the mountain to find this darling flower, somehow hoping for a sense of peace. She muses to herself, *If a flower can thrive in such harsh circumstances, so could I.* But she needs to see the flower for herself. To touch its soft ballerina-skirt petals dancing over the pagan earth.

The hike turns into climbing. Large rock formations jut out of the mountainside, and she reaches for them when the shrub branches are too skinny to pull. The path she normally takes up the mountain winds up toward a lookout where she can gaze at the peninsula surrounded by sea. She knows the path well—there are no snowdrops that way. She zigzags through ancient distal creases of the mountain. The heavens above her divine only hues of blue. The air is cool, and it feels delicious in her lungs. She is taken by the moment, and for a while—and while outside of her cave—she forgets the scar around her eye. She wears her cloak. Her unhooded head bursts with spiraling shoots of red hair. She is like a wildflower herself, and her green cloak skirts over Mount Athos.

Her mind is so distraught that had she not found a patch of snowdrops on her way back down she might not have come back home. She is elated when she sees the white crème of the flower she adores cast in the shadow of a boulder she leaned on earlier when she came up the mountain. She has spent all morning looking for them, and by now she is running late to the ceremony that waits for her. She plucks a single snowdrop from the ground and holds it close to her cheek before starting back down toward the monastery, as if hand in hand with Father Stephanos.

Anna makes it to the main trail that leads to the lookout, and there she runs into Sarasa. Sarasa and Anna have become friends by accident. Anna first met her when she was summiting the mountain one day in order to pray to God. Sarasa was already at the top sitting on a rock edge with her feet dangling, staring at them. Anna spoke first, "Hello," and this startled Sarasa and made it evident when she grabbed at her chest, her fingers pulling from one another like cells in mitosis, by necessity. She collected herself. She stood up and away from the ledge. A weak, "Hi," was all that she could let out. The hem of her white dress fluttered in the wind while the floral pattern latticed up her unflattering breasts. She stood as if at the end of an aisle, yet the sky seemed merrier than she with its sun dwarfing her.

Her face looks now like it did then, distraught. "Hey, Sarasa, what's wrong? Is everything all right?" Sarasa looks up at Anna with tears. Anna walks toward her and embraces her in a big sister kind of hug. Unbeknownst to Sarasa, Anna is, in fact, three years her senior.

"Tell me, what happened?"

"My mother's the worst! Sh-he can go to a Dead Land and die for all I care!" Sarasa now flushes with anger. Anna knows of her friend's continued tension with her mother. The constant comparing, the sexual prowess that Sarasa doesn't think she can match, the expectation of following after her mother; all of the weight of a female Dasein on Biome 1 that seems weightless for Sybil is felt by Sarasa. Anna thinks it is more of that drama, but a new scene. Sarasa steps out of Anna's hug, saying, "All sh-she th-hinks about is hers-self! Sh-he pretends that sh-he has my best interests in mind." Sarasa is thermal. Her head shaking. "Shh-he fucked him."

"Who?"

"Parnassuth!"

"No ..." says Anna with shock in her eyes. She knows of Sarasa's interest in him. She's pined for him for months now.

"Yeah. I even t-told her about him and she sth-till had to go jump on him, to go hump him, for the earth and shit."It isn't the fact that Sarasa's mother has had sex with yet another male Dasein in the same week. It isn't the fact that she has had sex with a younger male Dasein—younger by almost two decades even. It is the fact that she had sex with the Dasein Sarasa desires. Sarasa fears that he might not be interested in her, and yet it didn't stop her mother from effortlessly exercising her potent feminology. She feels robbed. She wonders if she will ever possess such influence. She doubts it.

"I'm so sorry. That's awful. How could she do that?"

"Because sh-hhe's a walking vagina!" Anna laughs after a long bout of silence. Sarasa can't help but grin. "Sh-he is, and you know it." Anna turns, looking at the direction Sarasa had been traveling. "So, where are you going?"

"I needed t-time to th-hink."

But Anna knows her *thinking* leads to ledges and staring down rockfaces. She thinks of how to turn her around and keep her from isolating herself but doesn't want to be explicit about it. "You know, we are both going to be late to the ceremony."

"I don't even care anymore. I don't!"

It is Anna's turn to be vulnerable. "I'm scared," says Anna. Sarasa's brows unknit, and she falls silent in response to Anna's strange confession.

"I'm scared and could use a friend there beside me." Anna's good intentions and her personal strife now blur together.

"Scared? What could *you* be scared about? You're beautiful. I s-see the way others look at you."

Anna becomes uneasy when she hears the idea of being looked at. Anna then reaches toward her eye to make sure her scar is covered by her hair and thinks of a way to quickly distract Sarasa from what she is hiding. "Well, maybe not all of us want to be walking vaginas."

Sarasa laughs. She feels such comfort from Anna any time they are around each other, and it delights her to know that female Dasein can be more than the sex goddesses of Biome 1. She always needs reminding from Anna whenever her mother is preparing for some ritual. Anna puts her at ease the way only a friend can do.

"Okay, fine … let's-th-go have our tea party," says Sarasa, rolling her eyes.

Buddal 21, 2996 has been scribed on an official-like document by one of the judges. It is today's date heading a report to recognize the new adults of Biome 1. This kind of information is deemed "necessary" and given to the Dublican for documentation for census tracking. It is only a formality to cast the guise of his dependence on their sharing of information. He already knows what is going on. It doesn't take him long to identify the religious habits of the land dwellers and send drones to monitor. He has witnessed the ceremony of Anthízo before, and he is watching now from his observation station with a little grackle-like bird perched on the roof of the monastery.

The monastery is teeming with male and female Dasein. The hundreds of Dasein who live on the peninsula all gather in the courtyard; some stand on the balconies; all have come to witness the coming of age of Anna, Sarasa, and Hera. Everyone, including Anna's father.

Athos gets to where he can see everything his daughter will experience in the ceremony. He feels without power or ability to protect his daughter in this moment. He can no longer keep her from this world, but he feels that, somehow, being able to watch everything is going to make it better. It won't.

Sybil stands at the end of the cobblestone path, the rotund building behind her where the ceremonial elements are staged, and the three females gliding toward her. She stands rigid with her chin elevated higher than usual, clothed more than usual, under such a pretty sky. Stranger things have been juxtaposed, but the gaiety all around and the bizarre vision in front of the initiates seems to manifest a schizophrenic reality that horrifies Athos when he sees Sybil. She looks morose with an almost vacant expression. Anna instantly feels dread when she sees the dark clay and charcoal covering her face from forehead to cheekbones. Sybil bares the triple goddess moons contrasting her forehead and flecks of white dotted under her eyes. Eyes that stare like a paralyzed universe whose stars do not know gravity. Her eyeballs seem to float in her head while she hums something that can't be heard over the Thrushes' song, "Bless'd Be." Her fantastic appearance concludes her standing there looking like the Queen of Swords with a regal confidence and elegantly postured—one would never have guessed her capable of sacrificing her child to a witch.

The three females take barefooted steps, one behind the next. First is Hera, then Anna, then Sarasa. All of them wear the ceremonial white tunics with white sashes they are to wear until the summer solstice. Anna's head is now one among all the others wearing earthly crowns amidst this pagan assembly.

Anna cannot believe what is happening. If she ever had an out-of-body experience, it was now. She feels like she can see herself, her body, walking toward a dark fate, while her soul watches from the other end of the cobblestones. Her soul hears the gnat-sized voice, but she will let her body move through the ceremony as she ought.

The three kneel before this Faustian-like tribe of witches. Sybil takes naked hands and raises them, calling out the name Eostre to witness and accept the three into maturity, the congregation of witches whooping in joy. Their shouts startle Anna. She looks from the sides of her eyes at all the celebrants; some as young as toddlers stand with naïve smiles and clap. While Sybil proceeds in the formalities, Anna notices something or someone in the rotund building just behind Sybil. She dares to move her head to look into the dimly lit building where she meets a pair of eyes looking back at her from a tall three-paneled mirror. The room inside is so dark, obscuring any chance of recognizing who it may be, and perhaps the lack of light inside makes this being seem more menacing than the noon sky above would have, but she feels horror for the first time. The longer she stares, the more gooseflesh she grows. The set of eyes seem to belong not to some waning moon nymph but more like to a bat chancing a peek from behind her wing. Anna discerns a female form, a twisting crown not quite like the others, from her shoulders tufts of long hair of some kind, and the same black that is painted on Sybil streaks across her eyes and the bridge of her nose. *Could that be her?* Anna knows of the Crone, everyone does, but she never saw her in person for she usually walked under a moon. A look turns into a stare. Those eyes could belong to a nyctophiliac and whosoever could only dream primordialist dreams. She looks otherworldly and stares with an eternal gaze.

Antania stands there, back turned, gray eyes looking behind her from the mirror. She is looking at him when Anna peeks over at her. She sees the man, Alexander! She stares and stares, thinking about the last night she saw her daughter, about how he took her away, about how the protection spell she placed on Anna was always for Anna's benefit. She had been enraged by

Alexander's unreasonableness in the matter. He spoke of God while she cursed him and the Patriarchy he clung to. Antania's eyes look down at the spiraling red-haired initiate who fixes her gaze on her. She remembers the fire. She remembers their life together: communal and unwed. It was a charming blossom, but a flower that was always for a season.

Anna moves back into place, terrified. Evil had seemed mostly an idea until she felt that cold, dark stare. Good and evil, those words are banished from the peninsula. They are so thoroughly hidden from all Dasein, everywhere, that when her father speaks about good and evil, it is like he speaks esoteric knowledge that belonged to old men shrouded in clouds of pipe tobacco. She believes in God, and yet the devil is nowhere to be seen on Biome 1. Not one feature of carbon is bedeviled there, but those eyes surely must have been plucked from the devil himself. An old-world knowledge lurks behind them with a dark history, Anna's history. She prays, trying to ignore the shape of them: large, owl-like eyes rounded to a point as sharp as talons beholding pupils as dark as venous blood.

Sybil takes a chalice once used by the monks, fills it with milk thistle tea, and gives it first to Hera.

"Paidí mou," she calls her, "breathe it in first. Let it awaken the goddess inside you. Then drink. Drink and feel your new life's season warm you from within," to which Hera responds with the salutary custom.

"Yes, Mother," and takes a drink of the tea. Sybil brings the chalice to Anna. "Paidí mou," she says, but when the chalice is given to her it has to be placed in her hands, unlike Hera who took it without hesitation. And when given her instruction Anna softly and without conviction responds, "Yes ... Mother." She sips the tea.

Athos winces when she drinks. His daughter, his flesh and blood, has been siphoned into some sort of pterodactyl dream that can't be real. His heart is pounding. Never has there been afternoon tea with so much at stake. When the chalice is finally given to Sarasa, she gulps down the rest of the tea and responds in her fashion, "Yeth, Mama," but her mother looks disapprovingly when she hears the 's' stumble in Sarasa's mouth and the cutesy permutation of 'mother' that seems only to beg for attention. Sybil takes the empty chalice back with an exaggerated pause and stern look at her daughter before returning to her place. Ambition, Fear, and Bitterness kneel before the Mother.

"My darlings, rise and be recognized." As they all stand, Anna looks over to see if the dark figure still haunts the room behind Sybil, but there is no one to be seen. They turn, and the whole assembly cheers.

The Dublican sees the roaring, cheering land dwellers jubilant and festive, and it frustrates him. He is in a melancholic humor, and the hangover doesn't help. "Three new almost-whores, yay." He scoffs like he isn't interested, like he is better than the religious impulses of the land dwellers, but his nature doesn't keep him from looking like a pervert. When he realizes Sybil is going to keep her clothes on, he goes back to logging data.

He sits in his state-of-the-art chair under fluorescent light. It is behind a sleek desk illuminated by the screen that contains what those little bird eyes see. He is surrounded by sounds of humming computers and beeping alarms. Metadata scrolling up a monitor that is being processed, calculating weather and atmospheric elements. Battery packs sit at the table beside him, charging for his drones—one of which is disassembled for maintenance, its feathers life-like. He types on a lambent keyboard, which glows only in use and is otherwise invisible on the desk. Geometry informs every decision, and Howard's creativity is calculated by maximized efficiency. It isn't as profitable to watch the Dasein every moment of the day. He chooses key times to deliberately watch. The seasonal festivals usually prove entertaining enough for Howard, for he is a voyeur who loves to admire the naked tendencies of Sybil. If his data were ever to be audited, he is prepared to defend his voyeurism with the intention to understand the leadership practices of the local Dasein.

Howard doesn't assume a lizard's mind like so many dystopians seem to do, but rather, his is a lonely and bitter mind. The artifact of his loneliness has been ignored since Sybil became the Matron. It is a photo of his late wife, stored on a memory key recently ditched for the alluring and comeliness of Sybil. She could steal the affections of younger male Dasein, and she unwittingly has stolen Howard's attention as well.

Sybil places a hand on the shoulders of Hera and Sarasa, while her voice sounded on Anna.

"Wait. You three come with me. Before you go and celebrate, someone has come to see all of you. Right this way." And she turns, leading them to the rotund building. Anna's heart stomps in her chest. She desires to go anywhere else but that building. Sarasa bumps into Anna, who is hesitating in her steps.

"Hey, you all right?" she asks. Anna keeps quiet and queues right behind Hera so as to stave off any impression that something might bother her about all of this witchery. She feels like a heretic. She doesn't want to portray heresy to the Dasein as well.

"I want you all to meet Antania." Sybil speaks with warmth, the kind that entreats someone toward reverence. And from a shadow in the room, Antania steps out to become visible to the newest adult Dasein. She looks at them all, but she gives more attention to Anna, and this frightens Anna all the more.

Once she comes nearer, where the spring light is flirting beside a wintery shadow, Anna sees the fur-wearing Antania with her chest bare, and upon her unfading female glory are cryptic letters painted in black. Sigils, self-painted and worn as a bodice between and under her breasts, they look like the bosom of a dusky seaside sparrow.

"You must be the Crone?" asks Hera, her eyes like she solved a mystery.

"I am," she says, still looking at Anna.

Clocks do not exist on this peninsula, but if they did you would be able to hear one ticking away the seconds. The silence makes Anna fidget, and she claws at her hair making sure her scar is veiled. Antania raises a suspicious brow. Sybil seeks to interrupt the silence and prompt Antania toward her reason for a private meeting.

"The Priestess," she calls her, "is here to talk about her vision." But it is more than just a vision. Antania snaps out of her studious manner and begins walking a circle around the three. She closes the doors to the room and continues pacing. There is a small container of some kind, apothecary in shape, but opaque and blue. Antania reaches into it and pulls out a handful of ashes, which she promptly lets trail behind her as she circles. It is the ashes of a child she spreads around, per the instruction of a midnight voice that called itself Ereshkigal, of which Sybil knows nothing.

Antania starts softly mouthing a spell of a kind, which grows louder and rises and falls between hisses. Sybil commands the spelled females to stand still. Anna is terrified. These pagan waters are as deep as they are dark. Sarasa watches curiously while Hera closes her eyes and breathes in deeply to receive the spell like a gift. When Antania finishes, she stands there with a Spartan's smile. She returns the lid on the container.

"What *wath* all that?" asks Sarasa.

"One of you will soon be revealed as the Maiden. Before the Summer Moon. And the Triple Goddess shall be made manifest." Antania speaks like a sophist. Her treatment of words as facts and her proofs are the incoherent sounds of her spell.

"Oh, well, this is beautiful news. Is it not?" And Sybil looks at them all to prod on enthusiasm.

"Yes, Mother," say Anna and Sarasa in unison.

"Blessed be!" says Hera.

"Wonderful! Now, why don't you all go out there and scout your future dance partners," says Sybil. She changes her tone from motherly to sisterly, as in the manner of a big sister arousing the lust of brides-to-be. "Get them hot and begging!" she calls out as they leave.

"Which one is the blue-eyed one?" asks Antania.

"Hera."

AS IF THE NIGHT OF
ENITHARMON'S JOY

Anna goes straight home from the ashen perimeter with a migraine. It fell upon her almost suddenly and it is a sensation she's never known before. Her father decides he is capable of helping her home, and she requires his bed in order to rest. Hers is a stair-climb she can't make and too exposed to the afternoon light.

Anna sleeps, not by angelic feet like she does most nights but by the bless'd finger of a sorceress. She lies in bed with newborn ashes still powdered on her feet. Her forehead is hot to the touch, and her father suffers every turn and twitch of her face. She dreams.

Everyday, polytheistic light shines upon the parterre garden Anna loves. Eyes can wander by neatly trimmed hedges, over the blooming jasmine, around the slender cypress trees, and into the proud standing olive tree, its roots as old as mandolin strings. Anna adores this garden. She knows of it well, but she sees it now with more brilliance. The colors are zealous in her eyes, and so she walks along the garden path to smell the earth and all its flowers now boasting. Bees bumble over the lavender. Rhododendrons romance the air. Geraniums as white as dove wings grace the pottery that keeps them. Divine.

Anna notices in the garden, behind a vert hedge and beside a fountain, stands some sculpted thing. Two legs, a torso, and two arms. It is a pale and statuesque shape of a man, decapitated and dirty. Farther down the path she sees more sculptures, all of them headless. She walks through a garden maze that seems to push the light up from the ground. The walled shrubbery runs into a mountain forest with maybe an hour till twilight. The maze opens from the mouth of an oculus of tree branches, a twisting and turning ring. Anna gapes at its enormous presence. The wooden passage looks as a giant's wreath wrapped in a garland of ivy fixed between two elder trees, hundreds of years old. The bottom of its shape stands above her knees, requiring her to hop up and twist over. Through this forest portal she goes.

An hour passes, and into twilight she walks. Meandering feet with no compass, she is lost. Lost in the goddess-kissed greenery. Disappeared into some firefly kingdom.

She hears moans, low and terrible. She advances toward them until the bass of voice is understood. It is her father!

"Papa! What's wrong?"

She dashes over to the tree that he lies against, and, by shaking and pulling, Anna tries to move him but can't. Anna looks at her father's face, and before her eyes, sees all of his hair growing rapidly. His beard long and stringing. The hair on his scalp thick and nettling. Leaves sprout from his scalp while root tendrils sprout from his beard. Anna is horrified.

"Papa! Papa! Come on! Get up!"

She pulls and pulls, but still no movement. He is only able to utter the word "penguin" before his eyes close and the earth takes him. Anna looks down and sees thick green moss producing on his legs. It swells over them and amasses all over his body. Leaves, roots, and moss cover him until he wears the look of a sleeping woodwose. Anna, kneeling to grab at his face, feels branches and leaves scratching her palms. Her father, was.

She runs, frightened. She stumbles over decayed branches rotting and neglected by the fairies that should be there but aren't. She falls, crying, onto some kind of agnostic ground since slipped into dusk. She lies there as a wild rose, cold and despairing the coming night. Fear counseling her, offering her a prognosis of more to come.

Anna hears ancient grammars of a kind being lifted from under the obsidian horizon. Spell-chanters making guttural exhales. The sound of a mountain lion screaming through the air sends the subterranean rivers of Anna's heart sprinting. The screams resonate everywhere. Yipping sounds, like that of coyotes, sound. She continues to run on the most readily available path she can find.

It isn't long till she advances upon some eerie figures that present like a high-relief sculpture shaded under harpy wings. It seems they are waiting for her. Waiting within the darkly thanatos-night are three robed figures, all of them pointing in separate directions. The two outside the line of three point opposite, looking far off to places only Nyx would know. The figure in the middle bares a naked chest that Anna has seen before, and on her chest, she wears an opalescent gem where hides a rainbow that glints from the glowing pool before her. Anna cannot be certain it is Sybil, for there is a thick veil edged in a silvery arabesque pattern that covers her. The nakedness of her face is only that of an upside-down crescent moon. There, her lips are seen, and she ushers Anna to come. She is pointing to the steaming pool where Anna understands she is to enter for some ceremonial rite. Tears coursing down her face, she shakes her head slowly in protest.

"But it is your flower," says the veiled one. And Anna looks down where freshly cut snowdrops float and send floral incense and myrrh into the air.

Anna undresses, as if by a possessed will and without the hope of a lucid dream. While stepping into the warm pool, all three figures lower their hands together and look at her with three heads. Their stare, haunting. Anna smells decomposition surface from the pool, and when she looks down, she no longer sees beautiful white snow-drops, but decay. Leaves, petals, and stems swirl autumnal; three heads softly chant a spell, perhaps hymnals learned from the yew tree. Anna scrambles out of the pool and leaps away naked from the strange chorus of necrobotany.

The three heads who self-assumed the airs of the triple goddess gaze skyward. With hands reaching, as if to grab hold of the moon by the cheeks, they begin chanting.

Nos invocabo te Hekate
Hekate, visus vinient et filiae tuae

They repeat their chanting. They drone on like scarab wings in perpetual flight. Anna doesn't look back. She flees. She hears their mantra no matter how far she leaps and shuffles through the dark. She feels as though she can feel their hot breath on her neck, and it sends her farther into a panicked retreat.

The waters are disturbed and the bare-chested one begins to convulse rapidly until night fills her eyes, sable and starless. The transmigration of Hekate enters her and speaks from human lungs, but when she peaks it is with many throats, both male and female, and its voice pierces like hairy owl talons through viper flesh.

"Anna ... Anna ... Anna!" Still, Anna flees.

But of course she flees! And when she does, Hekate-incarnate disrobes herself from the triple goddess and shoots upward from the female body it briefly shouted from. Hekate astral-projects, blue and luminescent, like phytoplankton buffeting in the waves. She produces in a naked female form and jettisons toward Anna. She looks like an aurora borealis when she bounds through the air, blue and green hues. Anna is halted by Hekate's sudden appearance.

She is scared, but a new sense of wonderment is in her eyes. Looking at Hekate, she beholds a female shape of Grecian perfection, candescent with the universe adorning from nape to thighs. She calls out her name again. Hekate proceeds in charging Anna to assume her birthright to divinity, beckoning her to come drink from her breast.

Anna cannot move from the ground she kneels on. She cleaves her arms around her chest and shivers. Still crying, she shakes her head. "I can't," she keeps saying.

"Anna! Come!"

Anna trembles under that nocturn voice. Oh, how she longs for the dread of Mount Sinai and its Lord more than this apparition, more than all the truths of the Goddess, more than the approval of Biome 1. Her heart swells and tongue loosens to speak the only magic she knows.

"The Lord is my strength and my song; He has become my salvation!" she recites her favorite verse. "In the name of Jesus, I command you to go." She utters this at first with timid hesitation, not knowing the repercussions of invoking Jesus. Surely, with no possible agreement between Hekate and Jesus there is going to be a cataclysmic outcome. Anna slowly looks up to see Hekate no longer postured serenely but with the beams of her glow being pulled backward into an unknown darkness. Anna is greatly encouraged. She wipes the tears from her eyes and this time yells out to the apparition with authority.

"Go! In the name of Jesus. Go!"

The specter's radiance then siphons into the black window of nothingness behind it and is culled from the forest like spoiled garlic in fermented fecal mire. The mountain is now reposed from the yowling night. From between crow feathers of night sky comes a soft glow of light. It sips onto Anna's shoulders like warm tea, delicious and soothing, and steeps over her. The light's radius grows large, and the darkness faints away. Anna opens her eyes to what looks like morning light. She runs straight for the vast wreath she'd entered by, falling through it when she gets there. Anna's eyes sigh, but her heart is relieved, and despite being clothed only by the hair on her head, the beginnings of peace are exhaled. For this odd yet precious moment, Anna does not worry about the scar by her eye. She is naked and does not feel shame, and the growing smile on her face proves it so. But all good things ...

She hears a turbulence in the air.

Wings fluttering.

She looks up at a bird circling overhead, then two, and three. Until at last, a great cloud of menacing birds chirp and shriek in her ears. They fly with pandemonium and swarm over her until she kneels again and covers her head with her hands. They fly so close that wisps of her hair are flung. Claws drag across her back. They peck, and Anna is thoroughly confused, harried, and alone. It isn't until she can't see the shape of the forest outside of the swarm that she wakes.

TWO TRUTHS AND A LIE

While Anna languishes in her dreaming, the peninsula relishes in a charismatic night. Strings are plucked. Drums are beaten. Feet swirl and kick and percuss over the earth. A special feast is had, and like every moon-born festival, meat is savored as a delicacy— and it *is* a delicacy. Dasein can't shred meat into their mouths every meal they wish like people used to. It isn't sustainable. In between feasts, substitutes can be had. Instead of beef, lamb, chicken, or game, a day's worth of fish could be taken from the sea. This habit has not only ensured a wealth of food for Biome 1, but it also gives the Dasein a wolflike craving. They might as well howl when their feasting moons come.

The smell of sage, sea salt, and peppered meat lull their months' ache for savory, fire-licked meat. Sarasa watches Parnassus from afar as he satisfies his lust for meat. He eats as if he won't eat again, and she watches while recollecting a vision of her mother on top of him. She vacillates between wanting to see him choke on a bone and wanting to see him looking up at *her* from between her thighs. She doesn't understand why she feels this. She knows of his many epicurean escapades about the peninsula; but even so, she wants him.

Parnassus is a hunter when the peninsula needs ceremonial meat, and he is a fisher when he and others have their belly-itching for flesh. He looks as wild as his vocation. He is strong in the chest. His arms have the look like he can push a buck over by the antlers, and they are covered in tattoos. Sleeves of black floral designs, florets of lotus in full bloom, a reiteration of tribal lines that are without a discernable tautology. Their mythic patterns become juxtaposed here and faded there into hyperboles of sacred geometry until at about the wrists—the shape of Taurus depicting the stars he was born under. His beard seems wilder than the others, like he snatched it from Pan's own face. The only reason the hair on his scalp isn't wild too is because it would get in his way on a hunt, obstructing his sight. His eyes are intense; perhaps he stole those, too, and from some Trojan warrior. If they don't seem to curl when he smiles—breaking his defensive perimeter—his eyes alone would keep so many away. They frighten and excite Sarasa simultaneously. If only she could feel his fierce passions made supple by her tender touch, she pines.

But Hera has seemed to key in on what Parnassus wants. The promise of a kiss he could smell but not yet touch. The flirty, undressing eyes that suggest an erotic prowess all while clothes still hang over a naked body. The thrill of the hunt. When *she* looks at Parnassus, she sees a Dasein as ambitious as she. She sees someone who goes after what he wants—and gets it. She seems to think that if she can shape his desires for her—letting him think she is the prey—then she will win over the idea that she should in fact be the Maiden. The power to influence is a prerequisite for such a coven.

Hera moves into Parnassus's kill zone by his table where he is eating. She joins other dancers in their jubilant frolic, but hers is a slow and sultry dance. She exaggerates what she can, what she is permitted as the white tunics and white sashes cannot yet be removed. Her neck is long, and it arcs and turns above her female flesh. Parnassus is licking his fingers when he notices Hera's body, and his eyes wander little from the base of her mountainsides, the cooked meat in his stomach only satisfying one of his many hungers.

He stares.

Sarasa watches the teasing and dancing, Hera displaying herself before him, and she grows mad—but she isn't the only one watching.

Antania has decided she will keep a close eye on Hera, having an intuition about her, and she watches the spectacle. She smiles from outside of the fire's glowing perimeter and enjoys the power of suggestion that Hera seems to already have; but she also fears for her. Given that Parnassus already possesses a sexual confidence, she fears that Hera might instead fall under his spell. This would not do, not if she is to be the Maiden that Antania is looking for. Antania's power and magic is as potent as an adder, but she has yet to wield the know-how of divining thoughts, and therefore she cannot gauge what Parnassus's intentions might be. She decides a protection spell should be performed for the ambitious young Hera.

If Antania could see Parnassus's thoughts, they would appear as soured milk ribboned with green and hairy growths of fungus. They would offend, not because she would think of him as a complete scoundrel, but because she would realize that she is like him in more ways than she would ever admit. In his mind, the Dasein world is a cannibal who prefers to savor the briny flesh of things and lick the bones into fossils rather than choose the honorable thing and self-immolate. It is this world that a cabal of scientists have become decidedly romantic with, or at least until the next heavenly body orbiting presents itself as the next lover of homo sapiens. But Parnassus is neither a lover nor a romantic of the earth, or of anything else, his affections pragmatic, his pragmatism infectious and implicit. Sure, he bought into the idea of unity among all beings and things and endorsed its henosis-like merits, but he takes full advantage of the mystical oneness in a way that seems most relevant—intercourse. As the bee goes to the flower, so does he to the vagina. His carbon allows for her carbon dioxide. He feels like an omnipotent demigod when he seesaws with the impromptu muse of his malehood.

The deity of Parnassus's mind cannot be discerned, but Antania has an idea. It seems perfect, and Sybil's petition for her daughter only encourages it further.

"My daughter, she … she hates me right now."

"Go on."

"She spoke for months of some male Dasein she's been infatuated with. She wants him. She wants him to be her first, when Kípos comes. But, I—"

"You've done something … you need a wrong to be made right." Antania speaks with a curious enthusiasm that sounds almost like an accusation.

Sybil sees that it is pointless to meander long to her query. "I was in the process of journeying to the Goddess." This, a phrase Sybil uses to gloss over and describe her sexual activities. "And Sarasa saw me … with *him*."

"I see," says Antania.

"She's timid, not sure of herself. She lacks the confidence, the poor girl with her lisp and all, and I don't see her being able to fulfill her desire when the time comes. Could you help?" Antania's face grows into a grin, and Sybil's follows suit. It isn't some sardonic smile, but the kind that one gives when relieved.

"Put this in his drink." She hands Sybil a corked vial of liquid. "And when he is ready, I will take care of the rest." Sybil looks at the vial and then back at Antania curiously.

"It's like you already had this planned."

Antania laughs at this but quickly averts the implication. "Hurry before he toasts away all his wine."

And Sybil goes.

Sybil finds a cup and fills it with more wine. Not all of it has been drunk up yet by the celebrants. Sybil sways through the very festive crowd of Dasein with the cup. The alcohol is working its old-world magic, and most have already become revelers. The others soon will be. It seemed easier for her to find wine than it is to find the words to coax Parnassus into accepting an unusual offering of wine. Her confidence is in remembering the way he looked at her—just hours ago—when she was on top of him. She finds him dancing with Hera by the fire that the dancers seem to gravitate around. Dasein move aside and offer the courtesy of acknowledging Sybil as "Mother." Even in their drunken state, she can be recognized. They can make her out to be a goddess if they want to, simply to pay tribute to her great beauty. The ouroboros of dancers slow their whirl when she approaches the dancing Parnassus.

"Mother," says Hera, but Parnassus just looks at her and smiles. He does not blush for things already done, nor does he salute her title. He simply looks at her with feral eyes.

"A drink for your efforts in gathering this feast," says Sybil, raising the cup.

Parnassus smiles under his wild beard, grabs the offering, and drinks it down by gulps. With red droplets of wine glistening in his beard, he wipes his face. "Mother," he says, giving back the empty cup.

Sybil takes the cup and walks away with a secret triumph, while the ouroboros continue to slither round the bonfire.

Anna drinks from a cup of hot herbs that her father has given her, and they sit in their kitchen where little evidence of them can be discerned. He is consoling her as she drinks. He poses playful thoughts to her about how silly Sybil looked, but her headache had not yet subsided, and the memory of Sybil's face is like a bad omen.

"Papa?" She hesitates in her following question. "Do you believe evil really exists?"

Her father studies her face before responding.

"Why do you ask?"

"I saw something, or someone—and then I had a terrible dream. I've never had a dream like it, and I've never been so scared." She grasps the cup with both hands and looks with large eyes.

"That's what all of that movement was about—I was worried. I thought something was different. Well … to the atheist, this was before the world of Dasein of course, I would always say that the devil has won when he's convinced you that God doesn't exist."

"Okay, but what if they don't believe in the devil either?"

"Then I would say that the devil has won, yet again, when he's convinced them that *he* doesn't exist. A world of doubters is a perfect place for such a devil to stomp around. I think he chooses to tiptoe now and keep the very idea of evil in the dark. Better to make devils out of men and have all the devilry come from human hands and human mouths. You see, it's the perfect crime—one that you can say you didn't do and point to the hands with blood on them. I believe the devil puts his will into others, by some kind of influence, and they carry out his designs. So, yes, I would say evil does exist."

"I think the devil is here."

At this, Athos's skin crawls, and his unblinking eyes stare at her between heaven and hell.

"What do you mean, *here?*"

"I saw the Crone today—that's what Sarasa and I got held back for. She has the creepiest eyes, and she has the kind of look that you can feel. There's a presence to her that makes you feel like someone or something else is there also. And ... she, she cast a spell over all three of us before we left."

"A spell?"

"Said that one of us is going to become *the Maiden.* I think it's the last member of their circle they are looking for, both Sybil and the Crone."

Athos shakes his head like he is trying to cool his tongue because he has much he wants to say. His protesting anything against this culture is a detriment to their lives. What can he say to her? 'No, I don't want you to do this'? Or to their society? 'We will not be a part of this'? Shaking his head is the easiest thing he can do in the moment.

"I was only ever worried about the second part of this whole thing, when Kípos comes, and I—"

"Yeah, I know." Athos cuts her off so he doesn't have to hear about her striding around public, naked, looking for someone to seduce her.

"Now, I am afraid that I might be picked."

"Why would you be picked?"

"I don't know. The Crone ... she kept staring at me, more than the others. And then there was my dream. I think she was in it too! It was so terrible. I had to—" she pauses and looks around, as is their custom when talking about God, "I had to say scripture and call out to Jesus in my dream. It actually worked! It was the only way I could escape from her."

Athos tries to hide the fear that grips his lungs and slows his breath. Fear mentors his thoughts, dark and disturbing. He has no truism for her now. He doesn't know what he can say to make the situation better. Instead, he stands and pulls her in for a hug. Perhaps she feels that he is trying to comfort her, but in truth, he is trying to comfort himself.

Heirloom clouds carbonate the early cobalt sky. Smoke curls from the still-warm embers of last night's festival, and Parnassus lies by it without shirt or tunic.

He stirs and grunts his way up from the ground. His memory is dimmed and he can't figure how he slept the whole night, and without his shirt. The greater mystery is the whispers. He looks, all around him he scouts, and no one. He is alone, shirtless, and he is hearing whispers from some far-off throat. They won't stop.

"What—who, who's there?" He scans about himself in a more hurried fashion. Still, there is no one there. He grows angry and yells, trying to cut out the tongue that slithers in his ears. He is thoroughly vexed, and in his agitation, he rubs his forehead from which he pulls black residue. His fingers are black as coal. He looks around himself again, panicked, and runs into the monastery, to the courtyard and into the building in its center where he knows mirrors stand. From a tall, dimly lit mirror, he can see some kind of nonsensical lines patterned on his forehead. They look like letters of a kind layered on top of each other, like a word written with the letters stacked.

He does not remember Antania's finger tracing over his head because he was sleeping in a stupor when she did it. She'd waited till the coronated fools left him to sleep off the drink. She came dragging a stick, which she used to dig a circle around them. She inducted Parnassus into her malfeitoran appeal to the Samodiva and any other resident nymphs that would oblige her. She stuck her finger into a pouch of ground, moon-cleansed charcoal and traced while she whispered foreign things. She felt rushed and hurried, for she heard others not yet sleeping. She couldn't be found out—they wouldn't understand—and there was much at stake. What is understood is that, when anyone casts a spell, there needs to be complete focus.

Antania's mind still rakes over what she saw during the ceremony. It wasn't less than two decades ago that she gave any thought to the Theron of her old life, to the Eco Revs that brought her and Alexander together, to the daughter she would chance to bring into the world. She somehow sectioned off and quarantined that part of her memory till the only thing that would persuade her into such thoughts would have been a face. She'd seen two— Alexander's and what could have been her daughter's.

It had to have been. It was her, my Anna.

But the very thought of Anna frightens her. She fears that, if the gorgeous young female was in fact Anna, that she will not be as effective and capable a Crone if Anna were to become the Maiden. She fears that a shameful accounting will be demanded for so many years lost. She fears that motherhood for her is only ever a lonesome memory. She has since hardened herself and made herself capable of things no mother should ever do. No mother should ever think about seeking knowledge through livers gored out and palmed and read like a book.

Where fear stops, anger runs. Running in her thoughts are the old feelings of that night with the fire. It was the night Anna was taken from her. She didn't run from motherhood; it was taken from her. It was she who was the victim! Her child was kidnapped, and she was left alone in a chaotic world.

Antania acknowledges the rage inside her when she troubles to unfasten the pouch of charcoal. She decides to put the very name Alexander outside of her mind. But Anna remains there, with the many constellations of freckles on her face and that mysterious red hair that doesn't seem to come from either of her parents. A daydreamer's trance seemed to cheat onto her face. Antania's fingers relax and untie the knot of her pouch as she thinks of her daughter.

When Antania was tracing on Parnassus's forehead, chanting her spell, she wrote Sarasa's name as a sigil in Old Hungarian, but Anna's face lingered spritely. It was perhaps the first daylight-thought under a moon-lit sky she's had in years. Her charcoaled finger was for Sarasa, but her thoughts and all her energies were for Anna. The image of Anna's beauty burned in her mind, and it would burn in his mind also. Antania knew this infatuation spell was compromised, but she had rushed away from the would-be witnesses that were stirring not far from him. She knew if something wasn't done to stop Parnassus, he would only make matters worse for Sarasa now, but it was too late. The spell was cast. Hundreds of years later, and witches still weren't perfect.

Anna rises early again. This time, she doesn't bring paint or brushes to the cave. She has come to cry and to pray. If one stood outside of those yawning rocks, one would hear a troubled voice uttering secret things. Things as raw as kissing lips. From the earthen hollow she prays.

"God … why have you abandoned the whole world? Why is life so hard? Are you also the maker of bad things? If so, why?" Her meditations start as desperation and soon turn to angry sobs.

"How do you expect me to honor you and survive this place? Is that what you want? My death? I can't even *paint* how I wish! Look at me! Sitting here alone, talking in a cave …"

She pines for God's providence and wishes to have more than a private faith in a cave.

Antania knows a little about the practices of oology. She knows little more than most Dasein. More than the size of an egg thus indicating a bird of prey, but she knows the speckling patterns enough to discern what types of birds will hatch. Antania cares not for the shell, really, unless it is for some springtime ritual. Instead, she invests her thoughts in the egg's contents.

It is the longest span of time she's spent among the Dasein, but the staggering knowledge of her past life made reincarnate to her seems worthy of her stay. She locks herself inside the small building within the monastery courtyard in order to divine the truth about the freckled face. She hunches over a plated crushed egg, and within the debris, a bird lies with its entrails loosened from its young belly. She pulls her finger from out of its stomach, slips her bloodied fingertip into her mouth, and closes her eyes. She waits, long and silent, as if to learn a secret from the carbon that will only whisper such truths. She opens teary eyes.

The sun's fire was veiled the whole morning. Anna doesn't mind the fact until she sees Sybil promenading nude throughout the parterre where she is busy gardening. *More encouragement from*

Sybil. Anna looks away and toward the earth in front of her, ignoring Sybil as she prances nearby. Sybil lifts her chin into the air and exhales loudly for Anna to hear, and she walks away with exaggerated sway. Anna scoffs. She would be there stewing all day if Sarasa hadn't shown up looking for her.

"Hey, what are you doing?" asks Sarasa, returning from her errand.

"Gardening, what's it look like?"

"No, thilly," she says with her tongue caught on her teeth, "your thash. You're kneeling on your thash!" The once holy white sash now lay dirty like dusty olives. "How do you expect to barter with th-hat th-hing?"

"It's a dirty business. If they can't handle some dirt, they can't handle me," says Anna annoyed and snappy. But it only makes Sarasa laugh.

"You dirty girl," says Sarasa, smiling big until Anna eases into a grin.

"Well, have you thought about who you are going to give your sash to?"

"I think I'm gonna give mine to Parnassuth."

"Even after the thing with your mother?"

"Leave my mother out of this—it's not about her anyway!"

Anna is always amazed when Sarasa speaks without her lisp. It is always in anger, and it is usually when talking about her mother. Anna doesn't mind her lisp. In fact, she thinks it gives a kindness to Sarasa, and Anna was more willing to befriend her because of it. Anna seeks to defuse her a bit.

"But he probably has a dozen sashes by now."

"I don't care! He's bathed s-since then, I'm s-sure." They both laugh this time. "It's Hera that'sth the problem."

"What do you mean?"

"You should have theen her last night. S-she was all over him. Man, I just want to hit her."

"Wow, someone's getting aggressive," says Anna. She is surprised by her friend's blasphemous usage of, "man."

"Just one hit, th-hat's all."

The two female Dasein laughing could be heard from outside of the parterre garden. It is the first sound outside of whispers that he hears, and it is pleasant and comforting to his ears. Parnassus stands looking at Anna and Sarasa, and his mind hangs upon the witch's spell, altogether confused but captivated. The wild nymphs of his mind laugh at his strangled will.

Athos waits until nightfall in order to go looking for the Dublican. He wishes to speak with Howard again. *Maybe there's a way to get off this peninsula and get away from Anna's fate. Surely not every biome is like this one.* He wonders why he didn't try this sooner. He wonders at his having to go looking for Howard at night.

It is only for great purposes that Athos finds himself wandering in the dark, for he is afraid of it. Darkness has seemed to haunt him ever since that night in the cemetery. He isn't an ill man, nor an insane Dasein. Darkness, and the things that creep and stir within it, have been a penance he's come to accept since he learned its name.

Athos seems to swim under a nautical night, traversing along the floor of some unknown depth. Fear for his daughter gives way to fear of every movement that sounds in the dark. The wind in the trees sounds like some ghoulish fiend moving branches to have a better look at him. The sound of the tides seems to bring with it legions of ghosts that come to flank him. Athos has to look up to the starlight every ten paces as if to catch his breath.

Athos looks back down toward the shore, where he is about half a kilometer to the observation station. He knows that he can imagine things sometimes, especially when he is fearful, but something is standing in front of him. He slows his walk and squints and pushes his face forward trying to see better. But he has not imagined the human-shape, nor does it go away. It does not move but stands, and very still.

"Hello?" he calls out.

No response. No movement, just stillness. He decides to walk slowly, the sand crunching under his feet. He needs to talk with Howard, and he is in that direction. Athos comes nearer, and by about twenty paces away he can make out a curious outline. The shoulders seem larger, like something is on them, and atop the head is something pointing toward the night. Athos looks up at the stars again for a little less carbon before moving closer. Once he has gotten but several paces away, he hears a human voice startle his heart.

"Alexander," is all it says, but this acknowledgment sends dread racing in his mind. Who could it be? How would they know his real name? Not even Anna knows his real name.

"I know it's you," the voice speaks again, only this time Athos keys in on the fact that it sounds female.

"Who are you?"

"Come closer and see."

The unmasked Alexander steps closer. The little moonlight lights the backside of this being in front of him, and he knows that in order to see he will have to step beside and have them turn their face toward the slivered almond moon. With each step, the highway in his arteries seems to travel faster. There is no patrolman to slow his blood, nor to monitor this meeting, and for once, Alexander hopes that Howard is watching with his drones.

He steps and she turns and the moon reintroduces a familiar face. His heart leaps like Anna's did when she saw those eyes— eyes that could belong to a beautiful gorgon queen. He has not said her name for decades.

"Antania?"

He looks as if he is having a rendezvous with a succubus. He looks her over and realizes that tufts of bear fur are hanging over her shoulders. He sees the astonishing crown that indicates more deliberation and effort than all the other crowns he'd seen. It sits on her dark scalp and above her now-clean face where once-blue eyes stared from. He looks over her moon-washed breasts that still wear her many sigils. He sees, but he still cannot believe that what stands before him is the mother of his child; she is now no man's muse but an unknown wild, and a thing only to fear. Antania, having gotten over her shock the day before, prompts the conversation further.

"So, this is where you've been, and right under my nose."

"It can't be. Antania? As in—Theron?" he asks again, only this time as if to convince his spinning mind. "But, how?"

"It's Antania," she says a little more sharply. She now burns with regret at having shared the secret of her Theron days, her old name flung at her.

"You don't go by your maiden name then?" he speaks in a subtle but jesting manner, now trying to calm his nerves with humor. The phrase, 'maiden name' seems to annoy her. It harkens back to the days of the patriarchy, for it was a patriarchal practice to have surnames and maiden names. The Dasein made sure that no nipple would ever belong to a "spinster's" breast again, for there was no such thing. Spinsters belonged in a bestiary of the old world. Marriage was disavowed and the freedoms won thus stand before Alexander. She looks tribal and undomesticated—freedom at last! But she wears a woman's form?

"This is where you took her?" continues Antania, disregarding his question.

"Is this one of your rhetorical questions?"

"I see you still answer questions with questions," she says.

"I see you are trying to follow suit."

Antania laughs at him. She marvels at his quickness to be crass toward her, and after so much time.

"Have you been brooding for all these years about us?"

Time is neither for Alexander nor Antania. It doesn't matter that he calculated the years by Kairos moments, events altered upon significant meaning, like Anna's birthday. It doesn't matter that she calculated the seasons by Kronos moments, like the weather that patterns the years away. Both of them have suffered the loom of time, but at least Alexander has had his daughter.

"What do you want? What are you doing standing here?"

So much time apart, there could have been much said if it weren't for pride. If it weren't for the hurt of, and loss of a child, perhaps Antania could have spoken the truth of her forgotten happiness with him—about how for the first time in her life she had felt safe beside a man and didn't wish to run anymore, that she didn't have to run away from the demons of her past. Maybe she could have said the truth, that he had her love, for what she knew of it anyhow, but the truth is a vulnerable thing. The mountain preys upon the vulnerable and she is not ready to come down on the food chain. She will trade honesty for anger.

"Do you still pray to your God?"

"What does that have to do with anything?"

"Do you or not?"

Alexander is so caught up in his anger, his frustrations, that he has forgotten who she now is. She is someone with clout and authority. She is no Dublican, but she is someone. *A king was a mighty and terrible station to trifle with, but the priest was not an influence to ignore either.* This priestess, however unworthy and despicable in his sight, could turn the judges against him. And if so, what would happen to Anna? She would be left alone on this ungodly peninsula. Would she turn in her own daughter too? He doesn't know her anymore. Perhaps he never did. Fear taunts him to recoil into the recesses of his mind where doubts and dreads stifle his speech. He remembers what Anna had said earlier, *I think the devil is here,* and the thought looks back at him under that twisted crown.

His faith is finally challenged, and in a way he did not prepare for. He wonders if saying no would be so terrible a thing when all that one syllable is for is to protect someone else. Can he be forgiven? What about Peter? He denied Jesus, and three times. Surely, Athos could be forgiven just this once. Finally, and with much delay, he caves under his fear. He asserts that he does not, in fact, pray to God, that he accepts this natural life.

"I don't believe you," Antania snaps back. "Why would I believe a thief? Do thieves tell the truth? That red-headed girl of yours gave me the same look at the ceremony—both of you are so dreadfully pathetic. Your eyes spoke the truth when your tongue would not. And—"

"Antania, wait—"

"And!" Antania continues to say. "And I suspect that she prays to him as well."

Alexander is embarrassed by his ability to deny God, and shame teems with fear. He lets that ghoul in the trees come and speak of fear while the legion of shored ghosts bring him shame.

"I must go," he says, thinking of nothing else but of Anna now.

"I am not done talking to you! Alexander!" she shouts at him as he turns and makes a quick walk back home.

"Alexander!" He hears his name being shouted the whole way home.

"Alexander!" This name was a secret for so long that he cringes every time she shouts it. He feels like a criminal, and he is prepared to run from his crime.

THE TRUTH IS A CAVE

Anna leaves the cave later than she normally does, and Sarasa bears witness. She knows it is her by the wild red hair untamed by the green hood she wears. Anna never spoke of a cave to Sarasa, and from where she stands, not even the idea of a cave presented. She can't see what would bring her to some lonely rocks. This adds to the mystery after Sarasa watches Anna's shifty movements and quickened steps. She lets this curiosity take place in her mind and relents from her wistful thoughts for Parnassus.

She waits till Anna is gone before advancing toward the rock formation. The boulders seem mostly uninviting and without the promise of anything greater than her obsession with Parnassus (besides the hope that he would obsess over her). Trees surround the giant rocks, which had helped to conceal Anna's retreat for so long, but not much else congregates there.

Maybe she was looking out to the sea from the top? The lookout point is way better than this. Why was she here?

Sarasa follows a game trail that meanders to the rocks. She reaches the other side and sees the giant rocks with an opening large enough for any Dasein to walk through.

"Well now."

Learning someone else's secrets is always more delicious when they're learned without permission. She looks around first and then walks into the sea salt interior of the cave.

It is after a short flurry of rain that Alexander dares to finally visit Howard. The other Dasein wouldn't be outside much due to the weather, and this emboldens his desire to gain favor with the Dublican. He feels that he needs to, and fast; but he doesn't want to chance the dark again with his she-devil now haunting him.

Howard is tending his bees, apparently to ensure the weather does not harm his hives. Alexander approaches, and as he does, he wonders what conversation he can strike up that will seem organic but also intelligent. Howard is not a Dasein much enthused about the daily lives of the locals, and Alexander senses it, but his mind is not a scientific one. What conversation could he instigate that would capture Howard's attention? He thinks of the old world—both of them have that in common.

"Hello, Howard. How are the bees doing?"

"Ah, Athos," he calls. "Well, the queen is still alive and humming."

"Good, that's good to hear."

"What can I do for ya?"

"Oh no, it's nothing like that. I saw you and thought of coming to say hello. I guess I'm needing some old-fashioned male company is all, but if you'd rather have some quiet, I'll let you be."

"Well, I got some time I can spare."

It is decided that a conversation is better had sitting down, even if the earth is a bit soggy. There is a tree on its side, and they sit there for a while. Alexander looks around him and not far from Howard's observation station are the dilapidated ruins of a monastery. He wonders what Howard thinks about such scenes. Howard lives so close to the ruins there is no way he can overlook them, and if he does, it would be an intentional disregard.

Alexander decides that a conversation about such a thing should be had that puts them in proximity to the topic of religion, but he is without a direct route to it. He stares at the ruins for a moment until the thought of something he has missed very much comes to his mind.

"Do you remember hearing church bells where you're from?"

"I can't say that I do." This is a lie.

"I remember the last bell I ever heard was rung on this very peninsula. Apparently, they didn't always have bells. They used a wooden hammer and a wooden board, and a monk would walk about banging on the board as a call to prayer. When the world was still indulging in capitalism and building the floating cities, the monks were able to invite foreign laborers to construct and fit a bell and bell-house into one of the monasteries. They seemed pretty excited about their bell.

"Before all of the transplants arrived, before the monks were sent away, and on an ordinary Tuesday morning … I remember it ringing. It was accompanied by singing monks. They began to gather. All of them rose from their beds and made their way to fill the courtyard where they always congregated. *They sang.* In my entire life, I've never chosen to sing as the first thing to do when I wake. Coffee was my ritual—oh, how I miss coffee."

"Amen to that," says Howard.

"You know, I asked one of the monks why they would sing as the first thing they do. He told me it was to push the darkness away."

"Perhaps if they'd just wait for the sun to rise …" says Howard contemptuously.

"Perhaps."

Alexander doesn't want Howard to think of him as having anything more than a fondness for art and history, and so he thinks it wise to justify his having been on the peninsula at a time when monks and bells still existed.

"I had come with my daughter, you see, in order to look at the centuries-old paintings they kept here. It was exquisite! Simply impressive. They kept Medieval artworks, relics of the Byzantine Era—*the Byzantine Era*—and I counted myself lucky to see them before the world handed the keys over to the Dasein."

"You seem disappointed with that fact."

Alexander studies his thoughts a little more before speaking next. He feels Howard's gaze now seeking, trying to pry into hidden things. He doesn't want to fabricate a half-truth but answer with sincerity without granting him full access to a damning knowledge about himself.

"Art has suffered so much abuse because of the presence of the Dasein."

"I don't follow."

"Because Dasein ..." Alexander starts but rushes to quiet himself before he blurts out his true heart and before he unrolls the scroll of his mind over the flame of Howard's vocation. What he wants to say is because Dasein—who were once called mankind—were once believed to be the microcosm of the universe; mankind was to be held on trial and the plaintiffs presented themselves like thunder. Their charges struck without mercy upon a tradition that had thoroughly worn out its welcome. An entire world-view and its patrons were turned villain and condemned. There isn't a shred of evidence beyond the words of the old folk who remember. The old world can't even be found in a history book these days. It is nothing but a ghost story. Myth. Alexander has much to say about the turn of the world. Instead, he tempers his answer thus: "Because the world of Dasein was not possible without revolutionaries having desecrated all of the world's art.

Old world icons were defamed and destroyed. Images like the Vitruvian Man were burned. The Creation of Adam fresco was graffitied over in green words that read, 'Lunga vita a Gaia.' Hell, even the statue of Leonidas was decapitated and eventually felled. You remember that, don't you?"

"I will concede that the revolution did get carried away, but they always have. We must look beyond those facts and contemplate on the redemption of not just a single species but the salvation of the entire earth. Sacrifices had to be made, yes. There's no denying that fact. Consider ... if, well you seem reasonable enough to switch terms for the sake of conversation ... if a *man* were trying to kill your daughter, you would intervene, sacrificing yourself if you must, in order to spare your daughter from such an end. Yes?"

"Of course."

"Well, how is it any different with the world? A world of fathers gave themselves up for their children so that they might live. I think it's the bravest act this world has seen yet."

"Yeah, well maybe if the world were more grateful for such sacrifices made. There's not even the possibility of glorying in the memory of the world we lost. It's hard to have a heart of thanksgiving if there is no memory permitted. There is just *now,* and no more looking at what *was*."

"What is there to glory in? The border wars? The staunch nationalism that discriminated against not only foreigners but the rest of the animal kingdom with their arbitrary borders? Or, how about the acquisition of natural resources? Nations that possessed the ability to do so sought out a glut of resources while ignoring the survival of other homo sapiens. And how did they justify their gains? Might makes right. All it ever *was*, was a might-makes-right-enterprise between tribes, clans, and nations. The world of man was always might makes right. So, I think the world is all right in forgetting such glories."

"Perhaps," is all that Alexander can respond with. What had started out as an amiable conversation to win a friend in Howard had become a debate that forgot its cause, lost in the passions of Alexander's convictions.

The conversation of art and nations dies down to an awkward silence of swirling carbon that drifts about them, whether by design or chaotically—and that is another disagreement that Alexander is not in the mood for, and he leaves Howard alone with his bees shortly after.

Anna is toying with her now not-so-white sash when Alexander walks through the door. He looks at her with more clouds on his brow than there are in the rainy sky behind him. He closes the door without greeting her, without any words spoken, and this defeated entry is more than she can bear.

"Papa, what's wrong?"

Still, he is silent.

Alexander paces around the room before he takes a seat, but the anxiety continues to stir over him. He always reaches up to grab the top of the bridge of his nose and gives it a pinch when he is troubled in thought. Anna notices this and waits for him to lean back and pop his spine—it is like clockwork. He says that he can feel pressure in his back and will take a deep breath before leaning against whatever he can to find relief.

But there's never relief for a lifelong lie.

"Papa, please ... tell me. You're starting to worry me."

Alexander takes a deep breath and leans back into the chair before he says anything.

"Where to start." He puts his hands over his mouth in the shape of praying hands and looks at the daughter he adores. It is *he* who is worried—worried that she won't understand the lies he perpetuated about her mother. He looks at her and sees his little girl, now a beautiful woman, staring at him, and he knows she deserves the truth. If not for truth's sake, for the sake of getting the first say about the matter. He worries that Anna's mother will attempt to speak to Anna and poison her mind against him. Who knows what shadow she is whispering from now? "Anna, my darling, I have wondered how to address this secret between us ..."

Anna immediately thinks of her cave. *He knows! He found out about my cave and now he is going to persuade me to keep out of it.* She can't take the slow build-up and tension, but more than this, she feels anger spark in her. She is prepared to hear him scold her about painting in the cave, and instead of waiting to be addressed she will step out of hiding from it. She would rather carry on the conversation on her terms.

"You found my cave."

Alexander's eyes grow, and his face tenses. "Wait, what? A cave?"

Anna is speechless. She looks away until the embarrassment of unwittingly telling on herself passes. "So, you weren't gearing up to confront me about my cave?"

"*Your* cave? You have your own cave now? What are you doing in this cave?"

"No, Papa. I'd rather ... never mind. Besides, you came in wanting to talk about some secret. Well, what is it then?"

"No, wait a minute. This is serious. You—" and in that moment he connects the paint he'd seen on her clothes the other day. "You've been painting in this cave, haven't you? Do you realize how dangerous that can be? What have you been painting?"

127

"No," says Anna with tears beginning to well.

"Anna?"

"No! I'm not saying anything else until you tell me what you were stressing about before all of this."

And upon this statement Alexander is absolutely cornered into confession, but it isn't something he'd prepared or practiced. He never thought he would need to speak this truth. He'd figured Antania had stayed in Thessaloniki. When he left her, he never looked back except to look at the picture of her from time to time.

"All right then. You're right, I did start this conversation with a secret to tell. Before I say anything, I need you to know that this secret I've kept from you for so long … I did it because I love you. My heart has only ever been for you. You must understand this before I go on."

Anna can tell that, whatever it is, her father is somehow humbled by this truth. She hears it in the way he'd quickly changed his lecturing tone to a guilty one.

"Okay, Papa, I do."

And with a hard gulp, Alexander continues, "Gosh, here it goes … It's about your mother—about your history. She did not die in a fire."

"What?" says Anna, now wiping her eyes.

"It is true, there was a fire, but it was not set by revolutionaries like I mentioned. It was an accident. You were about to turn one. It was late at night. I had fallen asleep in the bedroom, but I woke up not feeling your mother beside me and I heard what sounded like whispering coming from down the hall. So, I went to investigate. When I saw you surrounded by thistles and lying on top of a pentagram, your mother right there, governing the freak-show ritual, I was mortified. It was in that moment that I decided there was no way we could live with her any longer. Your mother ... she thought that magic would be what saved you from the world. It was such a chaotic world then, so much killing and protests and hate. I tried to coexist with her pagan fancies, and there was you ... I couldn't walk away from you and leave you in her care all alone. It wasn't until I saw her knelt down over you with a dagger in her hand and uttering some kind of spell or magic that I decided to make a hard choice, and that's when I took you, ran, and came here to protect you and seek a life with the monks."

Anna feels the foundations of her past shaking inside the small breadth of her lungs. She decides that she needs to get the whole story. "And the scar on my face? Did it really come from a house fire?"

Alexander's eyes are the ones now welling. He lets it out in a burst of noise. "I did it. The fire ... it was because of me. When I saw your mother with the blade in her hand, I thought she intended to inflict harm on you right then and there. So, I rushed over and pushed her to the wall, away from you. But when I did, I knocked something over, I don't know what it was, but something was close enough to catch fire next to the candles your mother had lit. Meanwhile, I was wrestling with your mother for the dagger. It wasn't until I heard your screams that I realized the room had caught fire. Oh, my poor child. I'm so sorry ... Anna, please forgive me."

"Oh, Papa. I have only known love and have felt safe with you. Besides, it sounds like I should be thanking you for getting me away from her."

"I wish I actually did. Anna, that's not all. Your mother ... she's here. And when I found out that she cast a spell over you *just* the other day, I was crushed. My hiding you all these years proved to be in vain." Anna's eyes are like full moons glowing in bright bafflement, and they shine through the cumulus fears of her father. When she looks at him now, she no longer sees a man to be pitied or a father to be esteemed.

"Hold on, you're telling me that the Crone, *she* is my mother?"

He had never practiced how to tell her this truth, and now Alexander thinks of how foolish he'd been. He'd thought his foolish days were behind him, but now, when he looks at himself all he sees is a scared fool. He has hardly confessed, and it seems to be like all carbon dioxide and no oxygen. He needs to breathe into this moment now, but how?

Anna is all sorts of confused, but she is sure of her anger toward her father.

How could he keep this from me? Am I not mature enough to handle the truth?

"You can trust me with the truth of God, but not the truth of my mother?"

"Anna, please—"

"No, seriously. How did you think that my faith in God was less dangerous than knowledge of my mother?" Her poignant questions disarm any hasty defense he can marshal at the moment. He thinks it wise to keep his real name secret for a while longer. It was an ingenious name at the time, his invention of "Athos." The revolution that had broken out into outright war was a swift action against all tradition. It seemed better to be named after a land formation than chance his birthname of "Alexander" as "a defender of mankind" or a perpetual reminder of the name and legend of Alexander the Great. The world had had enough of warring egos, of "mankind," of the patriarchy. Linguistically speaking, Alexander hid in the mountain. He didn't mind the falsehood of his name then. He'd thought of Michelangelo Merisi when he changed his name. The world had forgotten about him, but those old enough, interested enough, remember him as Caravaggio—the name of the Italian town in which Merisi was born.

Alexander will remain as Athos to his daughter, for now. He doesn't think there will be much good to pull yet another pillar of Anna's reality down. Her world is shaken enough.

"I'm so sorry," he says. But she isn't having any more apologies, and she leaves him there sighing pitifully.

She feels like an existentialist caught in a traditionalist's musing of martyrdom. Anna has fallen prey to a world without mercy. A world without truth. There is no niche part of her society that will accept her for who she really is or what she's about. No Dasein wants to give into the mythology of Mankind anymore. She doesn't think that Sarasa even knows about the idea of God. How would she? Her mother had seen to it to teach her about the earth. The soul? Perhaps Sarasa intuited her own, and its truth could be referenced by the winds from the sea, the bread from the ground, the moon in the sky, the jasmine in the air, the summer nights. What does Anna have to inform her of her own soul?

She feels willfully impoverished by her own father. It is now only his voice that says she is a creature and God her creator, and it is only a cave where she can express this truth.

Just then, and without conscious permission, the voice of her father sounds in her mind. *God's paintbrush is ever before us.*

It is her favorite saying of his, and he has many, but this one phrase had been coupled with such a pretty sky when he said it. It was years ago that her father couldn't help himself to describe the sky as God's canvas. She'd looked up to the sky ever since, trying to find those same colors arranged so delicately—and every once in a while, she could see permutations of it: bands of yellow, for where the shape of the sun disappeared, but below, a warm sky so richly arrayed that it cheated the idea that not a single cloud congregated. One color would run into another, as if a watercolor painting, while the peninsula would sink like bread into a bowl of oily balsamic vinegar—this was her favorite sky. Like most intuitions about aesthetics, it was an indescribable experience. It pulled her in and tugged on her heart in ways she didn't understand. She loved how the sun seemed to gracefully bow out of sight. It could not be seen, but she knew it to be there still. She thought of God in like manner, and the sky would encourage her father's voice.

She hadn't realized how much she needed those sunsets to minister to her soul until she realizes herself silently gaping at the twilight sky from her room. She lets the colors of the heavens soothe her when the comfort of her bed seems lost to the touch. She stares as if trying to find the magic of the sunset, but instead of catching a stagehand with strings lassoed around the sun, her eyes droop into a mean sleep.

She turns and flinches often.

Anna is sleeping until she hears something stirring outside of the house loud enough to startle her awake. It is a screeching howl that sounds very close. The howl is followed by a thud on the front door. Anna is so quiet. She listens with exceptional alertness at this unknown hour. It had to have been two o'clock. Perhaps her falling asleep early has given her more awareness. Maybe she is more sensitive to sound from skipping dinner, but it doesn't matter. She's never heard such an assaulting noise outside of her home—or is it inside? She knows she won't be able to go back to sleep if she doesn't check.

Anna pushes the frothy surf of blankets off herself and proceeds toward the darkened stairway. She waits, hoping that her father heard the noise and is soon getting up to check; but he doesn't. She creeps down the stairs. Every step is taken in sequence to her breathing while she descends. She hears yet another noise, but this time it is a muffled kind of sound of two hard objects brought together that issues from the porch area.

Someone is outside!

She rushes over to the wooden door and softly unbolts it.

One-two-three—and she flings the door open as if to catch a very rude perpetrator of mischievous deeds but instead sees a human skull sitting on the porch. The moon's glow is on it, and the empty caves which had held eyes once face her stare. She is altogether confused by the howling, the bang on the door, and now a skull returning a dead stare. Anna walks toward the skull, looking around as she does, and picks it up. She leans a look around the house to see if anyone is hiding around the corner—no one is there. She turns around to get back inside of the house and show her father the early morning curiosity, but when she does, she is then staring at those unforgettable eyes that she saw at the Anthízo ceremony. They are as still as a corpse's, and the shadows that keep them begin to move toward her with vampiric agility. As she fled, her eyes open before the shadows can take her.

Anna breathes heavily, her heart pulses rapidly, her skin is clammy, and her mouth is as dry as a lizard's tail. She is scared, tired, and thirsty. She rises up from her nightmare and slips on a robe. She heads downstairs to make herself tea and sees that her father is awake—and she doesn't mind that at all.

"Oh, uh, hey, Penguin … why are you up so early?" Alexander asks, hoping that she isn't quite awake yet but also hoping not to draw attention to himself as he bolts the door.

"I had another dream again, very strange … anyway, I couldn't—"

She halts her explanation to watch her father's peculiar movements, a little more hunched over and with a rigid arm that didn't swing when he stepped. It is obvious to her that he is hiding something under his robe as he turns from the door.

"What are *you* doing up so early?"

"I was just—"

"Come on, I can see you're hiding something. What is it?"

Alexander gives a guilty grin which fades quickly to a don't-be-frightened look. He pulls away his robe like a curtain or an old-world magician might have done. "I found this just sitting on the porch."

"Oh my God, it's real? No, it can't be. I was just dreaming about that!"

"Well, I don't know what you all dreamt, but I woke up to a strange noise outside."

"Yes! But in my dream, it was I who heard the noise—"

"And I went to go see what was going on and found this skull sitting on the porch."

"I know who put it there." Anna speaks excitedly and is in desperate need of the chamomile tea she meant to make herself.

"I think I do too."

"It was the Crone," says Anna, but her father is silent on the matter and retreats from the claim by inspecting the skull further.

It is lighter than Alexander wishes it to be. The skull's lack of density seems to prick at the frailty of life, and all sorts of aphorisms come to stare at him with a gripping memento mori face. The faint red hue on the face of the skull makes him wonder about the blood the skull he held once had; about how the blood that used to swim all over it was more like a pickling juice and the skull a hard container for the pickled meat. All of these thoughts tease out after he reads the cluttered, old Greek inscription which his thumb continues to sweep over.

"Papa, what is it? Those words, what do they mean?" It is then that Alexander wishes he'd spent more time teaching Anna to read in Greek, but all she'd ever learned was how to speak it. Greek is hardly the world language, and so it had seemed impractical to spend precious time instructing her in a tongue that was going the way of the Phoenicians.

"It's not all there, but it reads, 'The glory of mankind.'" The two of them look at each other with racing minds and nothing to say in response.

"Would you care for some tea?" asks Anna.

"Yeah, I think I need some too." Her father chuckles.

The two of them sit at the table under a hanging candlelit lantern. The moon is still in the sky but preaching of the sun's second coming of the week. Steam rises softly from their mugs and into their noses as they sip on their tea. Anna, trying to ignore the skull at the other end of the table, mentions a need for more chamomile to be picked and dried. Her father only nods back. His mind is still racing somewhere else, which makes the house really quiet.

"What was she like?" Anna's question slams on the brakes, which crashes her father's thoughts into her own.

"What?" he asks, pretending like he didn't hear her question.

"My mother, what was she like?"

"But we've gone over this before."

"Well, before you said she was dead, too." She pauses to glance over at the skull. "What attracted you to her in the first place?" Her father watches her look toward the dead head on the table, and only then does it occur to him that a skull on the table is probably not a good idea.

"Hold on, we don't know for sure that was your mother who put the skull on the porch."

"Oh please, who else on this peninsula would bother to do a thing like that? Who else is digging up bones to parcel out? Surely not Sybil. She would get her pretty golden skin all dirty in the process."

Her father places the skull out of sight by the door and returns a flustered look of shame and sorrow. How does a man of such faith as Alexander's become tethered to his antithesis? He is embarrassed by his past: not only had the globes of his eyes encircled Antania's flesh, but his lips also. He felt as if he'd given into living nothing but a carbon-life, and he's been stuck in it ever since. Stuck, and bedeviled by carbon's own mistress and Anna's very own mother. When he looks at her, he sees only small instances of any likeness to her mother. The frame of her eyes is the same shape as Antania's, but the color she gets from him. Her lips pillow like her mother's, and this worries Alexander a bit. To him, lips are a seducer of a kind. He knows well the seductions of a woman, and should eyes fail, lips can be sweet as honey and distract from the tongue's truth—Antania's was as wretched as a wasp's stinger. But Anna's hair … so red and full of curls. She gets that from neither of her parents, and this pleases Alexander very much. To him, it is like a covering of blessing over her. She has been made separate. She was somehow God's from the beginning whether Alexander liked it or not, but this comfort does not release him from his brooding over his past. He wonders just how much she is like him. Will she also compromise herself so thoroughly? But of course she will—that is, if she remains on the peninsula. It isn't a matter of if, but when. He knows of the kind of men she would have as lovers, and none are good enough for his daughter. The idea of her being celibate all her life doesn't seem an option to him. How could she be with all of the sexual energies that cascade the mountainside? Sure, she has a noble heart, but she also has a coveted beauty.

Her beauty makes him think about the intimate relationship an artist has with beauty. He never really talks about the natural proclivities of artists and their knack for euphoria, their need to not only see and behold what is beautiful, but to feel it. For an artist, it's not enough to witness beauty, but to romance it—only then does an artist emote and manifest and create as they ought. Such are his convictions, but he wonders how they are any different than the Free World's paganism. After all, his romance of Antania's beauty was as dark as the witching hour. And yet, his convictions are different.

Alexander thinks some more about her question. He knows that his daughter deserves the truth, but what can he say? That he'd lusted after a witch and that his daughter was conceived in a cemetery? How does something like that happen? 'Alcohol' is a coward's answer, and he knows it.

"You know why God hated Esau?"

"Why don't you answer my question first?"

"I am getting to that, now humor me. Why did God hate Esau?"

"I don't know, but I get the feeling that you're going to tell me—"

"It's because Esau chose the wild over God. He measured his birthright to be equal to that of a bowl of stew when his nature hungered—in which he traded with his brother Jacob—yet in the end, he complained of this. Esau wanted his freedom, his wilds, the earth itself, but he also wanted the blessings of a son. God loved Jacob because Jacob valued his sonship and understood its greater worth than that of a libertine life whose only purpose is to wander and self-gratify. I tell you this because I have often felt like Esau whenever I think of your mother. I was the artist who compromised truth for beauty, who traded discretion for a delicious moment, to satisfy my nature rather than serve my

God." He studies her face and sees that she is still interested in the simple answers of what, where, when, and why.

"Anna, my beautiful daughter ... promise me that you will guard yourself from compromise," but he continues before she can agree or not, "I don't want you to suffer the same heartaches as me."

"Well, I am now, aren't I? You've brought me to a place that is all contrary and in no agreement with anything we believe, and you want me to live in this place but not become affected by it? Is that what you're saying?"

"Hold on, that's not fair. I had no idea this mountain would become an orgy fest. It had nothing but monks living here!"

'How near to good is what is wild,' a man once said, but the wild had overrun the world and smote mankind. Alexander's blood thrashes at the state of the world. Rousseau's fancies of some noble savage instead of the cultured man have finally won the day, but all Alexander wants is the carbon copy of God. He longs for the Christ to come and save him and his daughter from this eighteenth-century daydream.

"Anna ... you have a choice in all of this. It must be *your* choice and yours alone. God only wants a sincere heart. I know that this world is cruel with their judgments. The scary thing about it, too, is that they actually think they are doing the world a great service in stopping their ears from hearing the gospel of Jesus. Your mother was one to laugh at Christianity, said there was no greater fool than a Christian."

"Papa, that's what I'm talking about. Simply tell me. How did you, a *Christian* man, end up with my ... with a witch?"

He knows that his sermonizing had to come to a close, and finally he must just tell her the facts, even if they hurt like truth.

"She was beautiful. I wish there was more substance to my discretions then. It's quite embarrassing, really. She was gorgeous.

I had never seen anyone like her. Her voice was a magic on its own, and I let myself become entangled in it. It wasn't long till she was pregnant, and I stayed with her for you. It wasn't until she was placing you in a ritual that I … Oh, Anna, I'm so sorry."

Her father, still a man, the only self-acclaimed man she knows is now crying tears she'd never seen. She realizes that it is she who approaches to embrace him when it's been the other way around for so long, and this thought makes her squeeze her father all the tighter. Her father's hand now entangles in the curls of her messy red hair, and she hears him whisper his love through her veiled ear.

Together, they forget about the floored skull that watches them with empty sockets. The idea of a witch haunting them from some tree's shadow is wholly ignored in this moment. Although they cannot forget about the desperation Alexander's faith placed Anna in, she seems to forgive him. She loves her father, and she tells him so.

"You are the only father on this peninsula. My father. If for no other reason, it is because of your love that I love God. I have seen what a godless people look like. They have literally and spiritually made themselves as bastards. Your God has become my God because of how well you love me."

After Anna speaks, she can see him coming undone by it. The tears well big and splash down his shirt. He seems as though he'd waited, for decades now, for validation, for forgiveness, and it needed to come from her. Forgiveness, she gives.

Tuesday is a day for tending to the Par Terre, and Anna needs to aerate her thoughts for a while. Yesterday's rains can still be found at the foot of the olive tree. Stephanos, she called it, named after the monk and beloved friend.

Stephanos is elder to all but the mountain itself, as if it were planted by the thumbs of the Roman Empire. It is a burly and rustic tree in the winter months, but come spring, it clothes itself and make itself handsome as an old man still clutching at his wife's weathered hand. Anna always greets Stephanos when she comes to the Par Terre; sometimes she stays and visits the old tree, but not today. She doesn't want to think about how Father Stephanos met his fate and the reason why. She doesn't want to think about the fact that she could meet his end just the same. She doesn't want to think at all; just feel. She wants to feel the vigor of the world in the soft green leaves, to comb her hands through the damp soil and let the granulates of carbon exfoliate her struggles away.

But the earth alone cannot console Anna. It is obvious to her, the extension of it, the logic behind the great round globe that spins at just the right distance to garner warmth and photosynthesis; none of it was by accident: the curve of the eye too round, the pupil too complex, the blood that networks between it and the brain too intentional to be born of luck as if by a mad company of typing monkeys. Nay, Hamlet had an author. So, too, did the world, but the death of the world's author is a tragedy only Anna and her father seem to reflect on. The world's ink no longer spills on account of Anna's God. Those arbiters and sympathizers of the earth-only seized all printing, stopped all mouths professing, and unarchived all data pertaining to a world designed by God. And yet, the soul survived such anarchy.

The soul was remarkably not for sale. The world did not sell its soul; it was too greedy a world to do that. Instead, the world allowed earthen mystics like Antania to become their counselors. Whether a fraction of themselves or whole, the everyday Dasein of Biome 1 were informed by the wisdom of witches. It seemed better this way: to fling themselves into the hands of an unknown she-devil than reside in the hands of an angry God—even if He was slow to anger.

The soul, even after so many ages, has remained a many-hedron thing, and like carbon, it has transcended the plane of understanding. The election of spiritualists proved necessary still, so long as their first love was the earth. Anna's soul suffers, but there is no counselor except for her father. No one else to understand why she should be so melancholic in such a time as this, for there was none like it before. To be female is no longer a wrong to be righted or a personage to pardon with so many apologies. Freedom at last! Yet she can't understand why there is more reverence for an elder tree than for their own elders, for they have become refuse.

She can think of nothing else but of Father Stephanos until she hears a voice call out, "Hey, you!"

"Ahhh," Anna returns. She looks up from the ground she kneels on and sees a smiling Sarasa looking back. "Don't do that!"

Sarasa's smile only grows and turns into a chuckle.

"What are you laughing about?"

"I'm laughing at you ... telling me what *I* sh-hhouldn't be doing."

Anna looks back at her, only now more annoyed than upset.

"I know."

"You know what?"

"I've theen it."

"Could you be a little more specific?"

"Your cave."

DEEP ECOLOGY

Normally, Howard logs data for the regional PANOPTICS field office at this time of day. Normally, his gut is burbling and his mouth watering for his olive bread to be toasted and plated beside him now, but his mood has run afoul. It has been years, and still he cannot escape so fair a vision of her in that white silk dress she dreamed of. A dream that haunts him still.

Howard fidgets with the memory key in his hand, opening and closing its injection port. He sits in his chair, bouncing his knee like a spring, turning from side to side, pulling at the back of his scalp with small fits of grunts. Finally, he stands and walks briskly out of the observation post. It is his suspicion that maybe he was caught up in a double-blind study and he will leave his post whenever he is getting too emotional.

Howard squeezes the memory key with a pulsing fist and looks out at the sea. It isn't until the blood is choked out of his palm that he realizes how hard he's been squeezing, and when he looks down at his now-pale hand, he rocked back on one foot and throws the key into the blue carbon that separates the land dwellers from the sea steaders. He is breathing hard, and his face rests in a scowl. His brows flex low on his face like cliffs, and the middle of his forehead divides like a great valley between two mountain ranges. His thoughts are even more inhospitable.

He thinks of her dressed in white, looking so pretty. He thinks of her face when she said I do, carbon-made-perfect. He never thought that her face hid a stranger's mind. *How could she?*

There was a time when the human form was a mystical union that even Howard dared not defame. To be human was hallowed and dearest to him when her touch caused a thud in his chest. *Oh, how sweet the days were when it was "us," when it was "we."* There was a time when he romanced the days when it was "them," but she wanted a cord of three, a union made more mystical, a marriage between them and God. Between them and a God who watched his mother die alone. Between them and a God who let children become slaves and the objects of a crooked humanity. It wasn't that he couldn't see sublime inspiration in the ruins of a man, but that he did, and such a cradle did not keep mankind from treachery. *How sublime could that inspiration be?* he'd wondered. Wondering led to doubting. Doubting led to crass ideas like humans as bodies, and bodies as an orgy of molecules glorying in self-preservation.

Howard's face is not objective enough to keep the tears from flowing, and this makes him all the more upset. He kicks the rocks at his feet, sending a barrage of pebbles into the water. After the rocks splash, he lets out a yell that bellows out from the pit of him. The lungs alone cannot wholly express his anger. He requires the full weight of his intestines as well, and when the blood rushes to his face, he completes his rage with an uppercut motion with one arm and clasping his bicep with the other hand while looking upward at the sky. Howard stands panting while his hair stands up also, this way and that, as if it belongs to some mad conductor of a maniacal symphony. He feels like a conductor who's lost his way. He is the kind of conductor whose virtuosity cannot be matched, arms flailing, head craning, knees locked above tip-toeing strife—such movements you wonder … does he move the music, or does it move him? The music is his life and his wits the conductor, or so he thought.

But a man of science doesn't feel like these land dwellers.

The thought leaps in his mind like a frog, and he seeks after it. He wonders, marvels even, at how he can be seething and injured, and after so much time has lapsed. He stares at the far-off floating city until he catches the froggy thought and dissects it promptly.

He remembers how she woke up one day with an unexplainable dream. By all accounts, she should not have dreamt up a vision and conversation with someone named Jesus, who claimed to be the light of the world. She told Howard when she woke, and he looked at her the way an adult looks at a naïve youth professing they know things. He'd chuckled that day, pointing to the golden orb in the sky, saying, "The light of the world," but she could not ignore the conversation she'd had with a being she would one day call God.

Such a curious thing, a modern to herald the muse and motif of medieval men, and after such edifices as Saint Paul's Cathedral had already fallen. St. Peter's Basilica turned to dusty ruins, the kind of carbon that looked too tragic a sight to even glory with I-told-you-so-thoughts. The world was rid of its Abrahamic antagonisms, liberated for any and all and none.

Modern and female: Howard's wife, and yet she was not mere possession of a man. She was not to be furniture for a male's ego to lay upon. She had a name, and it was hers to do with as she wished. But Sonia wanted to yield such a gorgeous name before the Jesus who could beckon hearts, and he could do so without the preeminence of the Holy See. She rendered herself as rightfully owned by God. But this God—the same adored by a cowardly Peter? By an adulterous David? By a man-whoring Solomon? A murderous Paul? Indeed, the same God who created them, Sonia worshiped. It was but a creature response to her creator, and Howard hated this exchange. Hated her decided nature about it all, such that Sonia wished for the rest of her days to be spent in a Dead Land where she could love her God rather than be hated by her husband. There was nothing he could do but watch her being transported to the former Isle of Man, where others in her region would go. She embraced it as a religious asylum, whereas Howard saw it as reason to hate all the more that which she loved. The last face she gave him was one with tears. Tears of pity streamed down her face, and her lunacy seemed complete when she asked him to join her, if not for God, then for her. He only gave her a dumb-founded look before she was ferried off forever from his sight.

Howard returns to his post, for there is work to be done. He looks over at the messy ruins of one of his drones. "It's the second one this week!" Another drone had been attacked by some noonday eagle that was more than curious. This usually happened when he placed his drones in autopilot and neglected them for a time.

He sits in his chair and tinkers with the drone's internal mecha-nisms. The wings are so thoroughly shredded that the only thing to do now is to salvage the inner parts for another drone. Turn-click, turn-click, turn-click … Howard lets this mechanical cadence lull him out of his mental torments. And when he is no longer irritated by musings of his would-be anniversary, he notices two girls talking in the garden on one of his monitors. Perhaps if his drones could not capture color, then he would not have taken any notice, but Anna's thick swirl of red hair catches his eye. So, he looks on as everyone looks at a redhead: with delighted bafflement.

"Why didn't you tell me th-hat you have a cave full of art?"

The question places her out in the open like a single doe grazing a great open meadow: unguarded and vulnerable to any predatory opinion. It's been centuries since a world of opinions could be grasped in one's hands, and an altogether freedom has been obtained from the likes and dislikes of a matter, but not for Anna. The world dislikes her opinions very much. Nay, they hate her vantagepoint with a vehemence; but the world is not a murderous lot who enjoy a pastime of torture. How dare anyone be like the kid with the magnifying glass cooking ants, and with a resident smile. If only Anna were an ant, whatever her beliefs were would be sanctioned, no matter what. She could believe that other ants should be her slaves, collecting foodstuffs suitable to her liking. She could believe that not only are there ants more subordinate than her, but ants that are best savored as tonight's supper.

"What cave? I don't *own* any cave?" is the only immediate response Anna can give in order to find out just how much Sarasa really knows. Anna wipes beads of sweat off her face and leaves a trail of dirt in their place.

Sarasa has nothing to lose in the matter, and realizing her position, she continues in coy fashion. She surveys Anna, foot to sash, dirty sash to the dirty and flushed look on her face.

"Look at you, you dirty little liar ..." Sarasa laughs again. How strange a thing it is for Sarasa, the girl who nearly flung herself off a rockface because of her many insecurities, to be strutting like a crow and cawing before Anna—the girl for whom many pine.

"Leave me alone, I'm working right now." Although Anna cares about what Sarasa knows and thinks on the matter, her very life could depend on it, Anna needs to portray a disinterest so as to remove Sarasa from any sort of power play she might be toying at.

Sarasa ignores her demands. "Well, you're very good! How do you do it-th when it'th dark in there? And what'th that symbol? I've never theen it before." Anna just stares at the ground, hoping the conversation will evaporate into forgotten memory. Sarasa kneels and drags her finger in the dirt as proof that she has witnessed all her art.

Anna pulls at weeds more aggressively.

Sarasa draws one line, then another, and then finishes an elongated 'P,' which intersects the two lines in the shape of an 'X.' Anna sees it and can no longer ignore such careless conversation. She takes a clawed hand and wipes at the image in the dirt before Sarasa can finish it. Anna does this with a surprising agility and then promptly pushes Sarasa onto her butt, yet Sarasa's smile doesn't leave her face.

"I said, leave me alone!" Anna stands. She looks around for witnesses before starting for home. But there's more …

"You never told me the Crone'sth your moth-her."

Anna halts her stomping off and turns back around like a cat.

"What kind of nonsense has gotten into your head?"

"Well then, why ith her face painted in th-here?" Anna goes mute, her mouth agape, and that wild muscle that's in everyone's face—hers is very still. There are words, but they cannot leap from her tongue. Instead, her mind races while her face grows whiter. She feels inferior … she has been outwitted by Sarasa's apt study of the face in the cave—the face Anna knows from hours of focus, the face Sarasa somehow perceived with a glance.

How did I not see it? Anna turns it over in her mind. *It must have been the paint on the Crone's face that distracted me … but then how did Sarasa see through it? How is this happening?*

"I think it's kind of neat that she'th your mother. You know then what it'th like to be lesther-than, to be not as important—

like me." Sarasa's smile no longer dances on her face, but a face concealing sorrow betrays its owner with a dull expression and displeasure in those heavy, drooping eyes. It is a human face, and like all faces, it, too, bears the image of God—and Anna's heart begins to flutter less. Anna's mind is stuck between a cool walk away from the sudden confrontation and a complete sprint. But she knows of the immense pressure Sarasa has felt and the paradox she is caught in: free as can be, but not free, not truly. Sarasa's desires to possess the thoughts of a male Dasein and to be pined for are not wholly her idea but a learned one. Sarasa has never been comfortable with the idea because this identity her mother encourages seems to have a prerequisite of physical value only, and its metric is that of the eyes; but no male ever looks at Sarasa. No one really looks at her with approval—no one except for Anna.

Anna exhales a deep breath, such that the hair hanging in front of her scar moves slightly. "Sarasa, I need you to keep everything you saw in there between us."

"But I was only—"

"No! I mean it! Promise me ... not even your mother is to know." Anna's hand is clasping Sarasa's for emphasis, and she pulls her in for a hug once Sarasa is contented to relegate all knowledge as secret.

A new wind of curiosity blows through Howard's mind as he watches the feed from his drone perched in a tree near the two female Dasein talking about an unknown cave. His interest is set aflame when the lisping one draws in the dirt an old but recognizable image. It is an image that had been adored by the Catholic church his mother prayed in. The symbol was on bulletins and other literature that his mother brought home, and he remembered being so curious, just like the laughing girl was, and it wasn't until his college days that he'd realized the meaning behind the shape. He likens the image to colonialism and Manifest Destiny, things that soured him like vinegar on the tongue, but his eyes are wide and now fixed on the red-haired Dasein. There is nothing that can interrupt his new object of study. Howard watches more intently through the large, jaundice eyes of his avian drone.

Whether by day or night, trees will cast shadows. A thick rapture of evergreens provide shadows dark enough to keep the wild, tattooed hunter concealed from all knowledge. The darkness by which Parnassus is possessed is an even darker shadow that hides his own mind from himself, and his efforts to rid himself of such dizzying plight is the only truth he know.

He sees her hug Sybil's daughter. The girl with hair like wine grapes, clusters of them rolling off her scalp, is focal and frame to his eyes. This intoxication is unlike any he's known before; such maddening influence. The voices in his thoughts give him purpose, and she is affirmed thus: *Yes ... her ... she's yours ... yours for the taking ...* One by one, the voices say it. It is irregular for him to hunt so close to midday, but the voices, when they whisper to him, his body obeys. He stares at Anna with eyes like obsidian, and his face is tense, pulled tight over his forehead, which he still bears the stained sigil.

He stalks her as she proceeds to leave the garden. She walks alone, and this fact thrills his heart such that he feels his pulse in his tongue and lets his mouth open a little to slow his heartbeat. Sweat tickles the sides of his face and beads down his back. He listens to the sounds of her steps and hides the noise of his.

Whenever there are loose rocks, he makes sure to step when she steps. He makes sure to silence any dead or decaying plant that might crunch under his weight. He paces his way behind her like a mountain lion, but such stealth is hardly necessary. He sees Anna clunk forward in her walk, each step careless and quick, and she treks on like she needs to be somewhere. Her pace alarms him. He wonders if he should fall back farther from possible observation from some other that she might be intending to rendezvous with. But, as he looks around, he sees only trees growing in number, and because they are mostly Aleppo Pine—their skirts raised brazenly—he slows his pace anyway, bounding only from large tree to large tree.

He watches her stop before the mouth of a cave unknown. She enters without any hesitation. It is a perfect retreat for any mountain lion, and this lion had lost his man's heart a long time ago. He looks around, reassured by the isolation of it all. She is now subject to his power, and his strength cannot be contended against. It is sure to be a crime against humanity to take after his passions, to take from her, and before the appointed time. But he sees it a greater offense to rob himself of his nature, and what little apprehensions he might have had are quickly chastised by the voices. *Are you not strong enough? Is she not good enough for you? Go! Take your prize!*

Parnassus stands there as a perfect, featherless bi-ped, half-naked and with only natured convictions, he unsheaths his hunting knife. He lets go of the tree that he hides behind and leaps for the cave. He crouches through the mouth of it with mammalian agility. He pulls her close by the dirty white sash around her waist and holds the blade to her neck as he grunts his commands at her. Anna's yelp is quickly muffled to whimpers. The attack is so sudden and defeating, he is like carbon monoxide suffocating the life around him.

Howard stares at the ravenous beast of a man shredding through the white robes Anna wears. She lies with her stomach on the ground, and while all of her womanly mystery is being defiled and defamed, Howard continues to observe through the yellow disks that color the eyes of his drone. Twice, it blinks. The lens of the camera focuses with each blink, allowing Howard to lend his scientific eye to the matter. The bird's head bobs and turns so that Howard can look closer—not at the female Dasein or the male plundering her body, but at the walls surrounding. He flies the bird closer and perches it on a branch that is shadowed by the cave and switches to a night vision mode that allows for the cave paintings to be seen. He can hear Anna's struggle to cry softly, and so he mutes the recording. One by one, he sees them all. The many human faces, the scripture enshrined by ornate representations of flowers, and finally, the symbol that had interested him in the first place.

"Ah, there it be." Howard only knows to call the symbol, "it" because it had been so long since he'd seen the image, he forgotten what *it* was called. Howard shakes his head as he stares at the image. He pans the drone back over to Anna. "Oh, girly, not you, too."

ECOFEMINISM

—Dasein and Nature sing,
Dasein and Nature sing,
O, Dasein, Dasein and Nature sing.

Anna wakes to this stanza being delivered across the twilight air. The Thrushes are singing the day complete. Realizing this, Anna is startled. She sits up from the ground with only her hair to cover her upper body. Cold and naked, she pulls at the tattered robes left beside her. She drapes them over her like a blanket, trying to compose herself.

How did so much time go by? Did I really pass out? Confusion and horror riddle her thoughts. Anna rubs at her neck and tries not to cry. She leans on her hands to get herself up, and when she does, she feels an awful pain, a bruiselike pain between her spine and right shoulder blade. A stuttering hand motions to feel her shoulder's injury, and fingers lift blood from her back. She winces. A quiet sob fills the cave. Her sobbing seems to make her internal injuries worsen, as if the vibrations of her sorrow create friction all over and through her. She strives for breaths that keep catching under the weight of her afflictions.

—And wonders, wonders of this world,
And wonders, wonders of this world.

Anna lifts herself up by grabbing and leaning into a large rock protruding from the cave wall. It feels jagged and rough on her palms. She tries to look at the rock closer, but there is only the failing light shining in. It is then she feels anger for what had happened. She isn't only a body pillaged of its virginity, but done so within her sanctuary, and for the first time, she realizes the cave's austere conditions.

Anna, hunched over with her robes clung to her chest, walks out of the cave—and she notices a large bird. It wears an arrangement of bluish satin feathers. Its head careens to the left and angles in such a way as if to push its eye forward. It stares at her with yellow eyes and remains still. She remembers her father's warning about the birds, and a chill crawls up her spine as she stares back at the grackle-like bird that seems all too interested in her. Her thoughts leave the cave and run from the fear that haunts them. She thinks it wise to have her body to do likewise, and so she flees. She darts through the trees but stumbles under a barefooted pace. Her running is more like that of a wounded fox, skipping and pathetic. She looks over her shoulder to the sky behind her. Nothing. She stops and gives a more diligent look. She hopes that her silence will aid her sight somehow—if the bird is careless atop of another tree, maybe she will see it then. There is nothing.

Her father stands on the porch of their house, and she yells out to him as loud as she can.

"Papa!"

"Anna!"

"Papa!"

Alexander runs toward his daughter in no time at all. Her hair is a cloud of red. Her face is dirty and smeared with earth and tears. Her nakedness alarms him. Her robes all ragged and ripped brings terror to his eyes.

"Oh God, Anna!"

She collapses into him once she feels safe, and he promptly carries her into the house. He lays her on his bed and lets the questions come flying out of his mouth.

"Anna! What happened?"

Anna curls like a bruised tongue and rolls herself toward the wall. His face falls like a landslide when he sees his daughter's back—bruises with green, purple, and black hues; several horizontal cuts slash across the left; and blood is caked into divots that circled in an-all-too-human shape. Someone has assaulted, cut upon, and bitten his daughter's flesh.

Anna can feel her father's fingers touching where Parnassus sunk his teeth into her
back, and she flinches.

"Anna ... who did this to you?"

Antania has followed him to the waters he now splashes in. She watches her mistake while wreathed in shadow. Parnassus has found a pool of water to clean her sigil off his forehead once and for all. He is staring into the moon-lit pool while on all fours, watching the ripples fan out to the grassy perimeter that holds his shadow. He cannot see a face, only a silhouette without purpose or understanding of why. 'Why' is a question he has hardly labored to discern in his day-to-day. 'Why' is not as important as the 'how.' How to find game, how to keep warm, how to gratify; these are the thoughts that preoccupy his evolved brain. And the 'why' to these? Purely instinctual. Neurons and chemicals and cellular respiration and carbon are all a Dasein needs to know about oneself. All other matters of self are left to the Self. But all he can see while looking at the water is his moon-borne shadow cast upon the earth.

Antania withdraws herself to the night, and as she leaves him the voices leave him also. Half-crazed and half-clothed, Parnassus rolls onto his back and stares up at the moon; because ... because when one tucks an arm into their chest and pushes away at the ground with the other hand and foot, one will inevitably fall onto their back—there's no 'why,' only 'how.'

He looks up and sees it as a maggoty moon, like a piece of cheese, burrowed and valleyed by maggot spawn. Its once perfect form, smooth and curvaceous, works in a delicious lyric. The stars behind it are journeying their distant, celestial course. He seems much enthused under that existential night. It doesn't matter that the spring evening is cold against his chest, or that his memory is foggy, for he is his own sovereign once again.

Anna wakes to the sun's light warming her face. She is in her own bed and in her favorite floral green tunic her father had bartered for from traders that sailed to the peninsula last year. She doesn't remember going upstairs or dressing herself, and she thinks of her father's intuition, his thoughtfulness, his care. She thinks of how much she needs him now, for she is at a loss as to how to proceed with all that has happened, and so she listens for any sound of her father downstairs. Silence.

Anna moans out of bed. She sees that bruises still claim and color her body as charcoal on a canvas, unapologetically contrasting her fair skin. She looks like she has danced with a clumsy faun. She feels as much.

She pulls a blanket after her and wraps herself with it for comfort, neck to knee. She opens her door and stands there a minute before calling out for her father. Still, nothing. She rushes downstairs as well as she can and looks in his room. Nothing. She looks around, and in the kitchen she notices that the kettle is not even warm to the touch. She opens the front door, but he isn't outside either. Fear settles in her mind and crowds all the kindness of her father with phantom tongues whispering, "It's over,"

"You're done for," and, "You will be found out." Such voices sound while she thinks about the bird that stared from outside the cave. She accounts for the rather low perch of the bird, for its eerie gaze. It never moved, only stared, and at her. It stared while the cool dusk of evening was felt on her skin and while all the other birds were nesting. *It had to be a drone. And if so, it had to have seen the cave, the art.*

Anna fears that both her body and her soul are found out.

Her father is like a golden promise in a dream, but what good is that dream if it's had in a witch's house? These witches don't much care for her father. He is an anomaly to them. No other male Dasein looks after their offspring as he does, much less called them daughter or son. It probably doesn't help that her father keeps mostly to himself, only ever humors the pagan culture with a resigned vacancy; like eyes glazed over, he is often absent from their practices. Body and soul, he is withdrawn and abstracted into the furrows of the vineyard where carbon and tradition agree upon the value of hard work. Perhaps it is because of the labor and product of his hands that he hasn't been challenged for his daily detachment. Surely the peninsula has benefitted from his work ethic, but Anna had benefitted from his mind's tradition—of fatherhood. Anna had never really given it considerable thought or nod until the currents of her mind had rushed toward the idea that she might be forcibly removed from her father forever.

Howard's grackle remained perched by the cave when Anna fled. Howard had taken note of the coordinates of his drone and logged it for reference at a later, more opportune time before flying the bird back. He is looking over his drone for any maintenance needed when he hears three loud bangs at his door. The scope he is using for his work falls out of his hand as he jumps in his seat.

"Arghh!"

Howard only ever has scheduled visits from his superiors from the ocean cities; not even the judges come to his door. He is not expecting anyone, much less after nightfall.

"Who's there?"

"It's Al—os."

"Who?"

"Athos."

Alexander has been getting too comfortable with his birth name that he'd forgotten his guise.

Howard opens the live feed onto his computer to see who is standing outside of the station. It is the Dasein called Athos behind the stainless steel door.

"I wouldn't be here if it wasn't important."

The door opens and Howard's eyes behold the moonlit Alexander, who appears as if he has some kind of drug shooting through his veins. His hands are fidgeting, and his body weight shifts from one foot to the other. It looks impossible for him to stand still.

"Athos, what's wrong?"

"It's my daughter. I need your help."

"Ah, yes."

"What do you mean, yes?"

Howard, realizing the oddity of his reaction, invites Alexander into the station to talk more on the point. "Come, it's damned chippy out. Let's talk inside." Howard leads Alexander away from the workstation where all the drones are either receiving maintenance or being stored, and they go into a lounge area. "Please, take a seat."

"No, I think I'll stand, thank you."

"Your daughter?" says Howard after a bout of silence and staring has passed between them. He can see the uncomfortableness of Alexander's mind when he begins to pace. He must have paced a half-dozen times across the room before continuing their conversation.

"She's been raped."

Howard searches the muscles in his face to exercise surprise, but can't.

"I mean, brutally raped!"

"Athos, I'm so sorry to hear that." *Words will have to do*, Howard thinks.

"I need your help. I need to find the one they call Parnassus. He's the one that raped her. He is definitely no man, but all Dasein."

Howard grows more detached from this situation after hearing Alexander's last phrase, and a sudden link is made in Howard's mind. The monks and church bells of Alexander's thoughts had made their way into his daughter's art, and it is in that moment he realizes that he is staring at a remnant of the past, a patriarchal parasite, a fool of fools. A sudden grin stretches across Howard's face that silences Alexander.

"You should know that your daughter is in more trouble than you realize. I know about it. I've seen it."

"Seen what?"

"Come on, Athos ... don't pretend you don't know about it. Your daughter's cave."

If only Alexander could see just how black Howard's thoughts were, he would have stricken his too many words shared from the curl of his tongue all those conversations before.

Howard's wild energies of thought rage in a primordial sky and drink from subterranean waters so as to revive a hungry, Saturn-like kind of mind; and like that cannibal, it isn't the salty taste or the cathartic tearing of flesh that entices, but fear. Howard fears the import of Christianity above all other religious sentiments because he's seen how succumbing and affecting its sermons are. It's a tamarisk tree kind of religion: when the fires of annihilation rage against it, its own persecution and death tempt even more tamarisk trees to sprout in its place.

"You know, being that your daughter has already suffered, it would seem too inhospitable of me to meet her with a punishment so severe as her offense warrants," Howard now stands to lock eyes with Alexander like a man squaring up for a fight. "But as for you, and as the Dublican, I cannot ignore your terrible influence upon your daughter. The damned thing about all this is I like you, Athos, I really do. But you cannot go on in your religious sympathies as you have. Now get out of my sight so I can think of what must be done." Howard has the budding of an idea, but he will wait till morning to let it bloom properly.

The sunlight is high up on the trees, yet their trunks still wear the night when Anna wakes to an empty house. Antania can see Anna on her porch from within the robes of a Bosnian Pine. The tree twists and turns like a whirlwind, much like the crown Antania wears, and from the irregular and winding tree she calls out to her.

"Anna … Anna." Her voice carries on the air like an owl's hoot echoing over an ocean tide. Anna is walking around the house when she hears her name being called, but it is not her father's voice, nor is it Sarasa's—and this fact scares her. Anna, motion-less, looks toward the direction she heard her name issue from, but a stone's throw away. The voice calls out again.

Anna is still very much rattled by the previous day, and had the voice been a masculine one, she certainly would have run and bolted the door behind her. Instead, Anna wraps her blanket tight against herself and, hunching into crossed arms, bracing against the cool of the morning, she waits for the voice. Her thoughts mount upon the prenotion of who might stalk her in the wood-line. Anna thinks about the skull that had arrived on the porch and the suspicions both she and her father had about its giver; she thinks how the voice might also belong to her. It is a twenty-one-year-old mystery that will only have the power to distract her from her present suffering, but the memory of the Crone's foreboding stare is menacing to Anna's resolve to stay and look for this earthen witch.

Antania stares at the redheaded female incredulously. The Crone requires help from the tree in order to stand tall. It seems there is no other opportunity like this for Antania to quietly meet with her daughter. A private conversation. A personal introduc-tion. A chance to know.

"Wait!" Antania quickens to say when she notices the redhead make a start back to the porch. She pushes off of the tree to help the strained effort toward the redhead.

Anna hears branches move, and when she turns back, she has to squint through the morning light making its way through the boughs and leaves. Anna steps closer—out of the early light shining on her face—to where she might see, and there, she sees the familiar contour that had given her fright once before protruding out of the trees.

It's her!

Anna pulls tighter on her blanket until her hands become fists. She remains where she is and lets the Crone come to her. Gliding toward Anna is a wild thing, a permutation of female-kind, of what Anna could be, and the thought that Anna had come from this feral woman strikes her with fresh fears. Standing before Anna is a woman who's lost her way into the wild, and wild she's become. The Crone stands with one hand inside her fur coat, the other clasping the bear skins against her breasts to keep warm—this seems a human thing to do, but even animals seek warmth. Then there is the streak of tears that course downward from her eyes, unveiling her skin from under the blackness smeared across her face—but tears were something even the Dasein are capable of.

"My child."

Anna looks with more intent, trying to see the face painted in the cave in the face now in front of her, but even with full knowledge of who stands there, all she can see is the Crone. Perhaps it is the choice aesthetic she is garbed in, yet even when she tries to ignore Antania's ensemble, her face looks only as a grimoire to Anna and hardly anything motherly. And those terrible eyes! Even in daylight they seem ghoulish. They are as gray skies that have seen many a terrible thing, and her gaze is as focused as a wolf on the hunt. Anna avoids her stare as often as she can; only looking into those brooding skies when she speaks.

"Just look at you! And that hair, so red. Where it came from was always a mystery." Antania motions a hand to pull the curtain of hair away from the corner of Anna's eye to see what has become of her face.

"Mmmhmm."

Anna pulls away to let the hair fall back on her naked scar.

"So, Anna, you know the truth?"

"Yes, I know who you are."

"No, no, you know that I gave you your name. What has your father told you about me?" Antania had emphasized the word 'father' with lips and teeth like tectonic plates colliding.

"He told me about the night of the fire, about what you were doing to me."

"Hah, your father doesn't even know what I was doing that night."

"Then tell me." Anna thinks at least some good could come from knowing both sides, of getting the complete picture of her family's terrible past.

"Oh Anna, I only wanted to protect you. You don't know what it was like then, with all of the chaos and revolution around you. Men were absolute wretches—"

"My father is a good man!" Anna proclaims. Anna's courage is growing, so long as she can pretend the Crone to be merely a dirty Dasein in need of a bath.

"You should be so lucky. The world of men was an evil place, a chaotic place. Their abuse was upon every woman, every child, even the earth itself suffered great abuse. The earth was manipulated, used, and left in ruins everywhere man went. My child, you never knew that world, and for that I am so thankful."

"My father brought me to this place after that night … it was a place with nothing but men. I was the only female here. I could have been taken advantage of, but instead I grew to know the kindness of men. I grew to know the love of my father," Anna pauses and stumbles into her next thought as she recalls Stephanos. "I grew up here knowing great friendship."

"Your good-man-of-a-father, don't forget, stole you away from me! He kidnapped you!" Antania shows her teeth when she speaks of it.

"Because you were casting some spell over me."

Antania laughs at her daughter's retort. "Well, much good it did, huh? Him taking you from me. But ... what of magic do you oppose?"

Anna can see her mother's face is now dried of her tears. The conversation has come to confront her private faith, and a great swell of blood rushes into her throat and seems to seize her tongue. It isn't a conversation with a naïve Sarasa but with the peninsula's own priestess. She prays a silent prayer for help, for a way out from answering honestly.

An awkward bout of silence stands between them.

"Well?" asks her mother.

The silence between them allows for both to hear the starting song of the Thrushes lift in the air. Anna can't have been more pleased to hear them singing. It is for most a method of marking time and a call to seize the day, and Anna is prepared to oblige it.

"I need to go ready myself for my work now." Anna proceeds to step away.

"Your *good* father, he's the one that gave you that scar. I've never hurt you once."

"I've got to go," is all Anna can say and walks back to the house. She feels like her insides are microwaved while her skin is cold to the touch. The many shades of fear she'd felt swarm in her mind, and the sudden jolt of anger she feels toward her mother surprises her. She's never had a reason to feel defensive about her father until now. She is angry because her mother is right about her scar—and perhaps if her father hadn't already told her about the fire she would have felt differently—but his honesty, his good heart is all she counts. Antania's voice is just as suspicious as her eyes and leaves Anna doubting whatever credible claims she might make.

When Anna reaches the porch, she looks behind her to see if her mother is still standing there. She is gone. Anna locks the door behind her anyway. She takes long, drawn-out steps up to her room and lies back down in her bed, the blanket still wrapped around her. She cries herself into a dull, numb sleep.

Loud and continuous banging wakes her from her dreamless doze.

"Anna! Anna! Anna, you need to open the door."

Anna notices the sun has moved in the sky, notices that she has slept for hours now.

"Anna!" She recognizes Sarasa's voice and, despite the panic in her tone, assumes it is about her not tending to the Par Terre yet. Sarasa's banging on the door continues as Anna slinks down the stairs.

"Hold on! I'm coming!"

Anna opens the door to a very dismayed Sarasa, and they exchange confused looks.

"What is all the fuss about?" asked Anna.

"Why are you wearing a green tunic? Sarasa asks while she pushes herself in to close the door on anyone who might see Anna dressed so. "You should be wearing your white robe. If anyone sees you—"

"I know, I know. But why are you here? Why are you banging on the door?"

"It'th Athoth. He'th-in trouble, and Parnassuth too! I think th-hey're goin to get th-he chamber."

"What? Where?" asks Anna before her breath abandons her lungs.

"Apparently your fath-her thtarted a fight thith-morning and now th-hey are both covered in blood and being wath-ched at the theremony building until the Dublican ariveths."

"Come on, let's go!" says Anna after shrouding herself with a white robe she's pulled from a closet.

The old monastery hums with Dasein life. There hasn't been this much commotion seen since the pyro-murderer of Biome 1 who was also brought to the monastery to stand trial. The Dasein had hooted in celebration of the verdict when one of their own was cast away as a traitor and ecological harmony was restored. But these Dasein, Parnassus and Alexander, they appear like perfect brutes of the old world: bloodied noses and purpled lips, eye-sockets darkened as if by a midnight sky; the hair on their scalps greased with plasma and clotted blood; and their knuckles gored by the dozens of impacts of bone against bone. Parnassus flexes his detained body and grunts at whoever approaches him with foul looks. Alexander stands with downcast eyes looking at the ropes binding his wrists together like a criminal.

The first thing Anna looks for when she arrives is the chamber. "The Necrosis Chamber," as it is called. She's only ever seen its use once, and she remembers the horror on the face of its occupant when he was finally released. She remembers the Dublican was there, too. He'd used his chamber to punish Dasein for crimes against other Dasein, sometimes even for what he thought to be abuse to the environment. Anna is relieved when she can't find the chamber, but she is in a panic when she doesn't see her father right away.

She draws closer to the crowd and sees him standing beside Parnassus and encircled by Dasein tongues laughing, joking, and mocking the pair as criminals glossed in their own blood. Anna's heart thuds and falls heavy into her gut.

"No! God, no!" she mutters before advancing closer, hoping to get where he can see her. Sarasa follows after her and grabs Anna's hand, and the two stand as confidants, leaning on the other.

"Why would Athoth want to hurt Parnassuth?"

But Anna cannot form the words, nor will she try. Her lip trembling, she only shakes her head and waits for her father's eyes to lift.

The judges sit in their seats, which appear as thrones, and Anna can see them talking to one another quietly under the clamoring Dasein voices. She sees the stones laying on a platter before the judges and cannot hear Sarasa's voice while she stares at them. She has seen stones like those before piled onto one another in careful deliberation, each rock acting as a trapeze artist. Balancing rocks is a fun tradition that the youth play at. It is a craft that attracts girls and boys, and together they'd find new and interesting places to stand up towers and cathedrals of stones over boulders and beside streams; some are so talented as to balance rocks like a bridge over creeks. Anna had enjoyed the little rock kingdoms built by adolescent Dasein, but not these rocks. They look identical in their roundness and smoothness, but they have a different purpose altogether.

"Anna! Look! He's here."

The Dublican walks from the colonnade of trees and into the monastery, and a gradual hush comes over the Dasein. The Dublican's presence is limited among the Dasein that, for most, when he is seen it is only to oversee and assist in rendering punitive actions. He is not a hideous or snarling kind of Dasein, but the terrible business he officiates makes him something to fear. The Dasein eyes watch him closely to see how he is looking at the detained—will this Zeus be merciful or vengeful?

The Dublican is offered a place to sit beside the three judges, and Anna sees the contrary and strange convictions of these authorities side by side. The judges are garbed in ornate robes of wool and linen. On their shoulders they wear leaves sewn together and hung like garlands. The two female judges wear spring flowers in their hair, and the male judge has tied flowers at the ends of his beard like tassels. The Dublican sits beside the judges wearing the same suit worn by the scientists of the floating cities: an athletic cut of suit, with a mandarin collar, its very color changes with respect to the amount of UV encountered in the atmosphere, and his feet are wrapped in some kind of unknown synthetic shoe. The photon dyes allow his suit to be rendered blue beside the earth-tone robes. The fact of their seating arrangement seems the only clue that they share a common goal. They look to be from different worlds, but they all bear the same amount of carbon as earthlings do.

"Let us begin." Short and to the point, the Dublican wishes to execute judgment as quickly as possible.

A hand is motioned at the Dasein standing watch over the detained, and the guards push Parnassus and Alexander toward the judges. The two stop before the circle of water separating them from the judges.

Alexander and Howard lock eyes, and below Howard's is a grin. Alexander looks into the face of the judges and sees eyes of stoic tradition, dispassionate and aloof. The male judge begins to inquire the detained.

"Tell me now, who are you brutes? And why have you come to us dressed in each other's blood?"

"I am, Athos." He looks over at his adversary, standing in quiet defiance.

"And you are?" the judge prods.

"The founder of your feasts. Come on you old fool, you know who I am." The judges all look at one another with faces like great stooping mountains. The Dasein horde yells out his name in his stead and curse it as they do.

"Quiet! All of you!" the eldest female judge by the name Nova speaks out. "Give us your testimony, Parnassus. But before you do, do you swear to tell the truth, the whole truth, and nothing but the truth according to all that is?" Just then, a bowl of soil is maneuvered in front of him, and Nova gives a nod as command to observe their decorum. Parnassus reaches into the bowl and pulls out a fistful of dirt and shakes it in front of them.

"Well, what is your story?"

Parnassus looks at them all with dead eyes.

"Are you not going to speak for yourself?" It is after a long bout of silent protest that Nova then directs the oath of truth to Alexander.

He remembers the words of Jesus and the warning about oaths, a command against swearing by any created thing. He's compromised on matters far worse, but he is tired of compromise, of hiding behind the worn-out excuse of protecting his daughter. If God created every bit of carbon, does he not deserve recognition for that? Why then should one swear truth to another created thing? These thoughts strike him so that he cannot ignore them. Maybe it is his sense that his time is up on Biome 1. Maybe it is the blood he can taste in his mouth that finally pushes him to revolt against the dogmas of the Free World. Maybe it is the awareness that his daughter is standing in the crowd somewhere, watching him, and he knows that if ever there was a time to demonstrate faith, it is now, for her, and before their society. All of these maybes give Alexander a steely resolve to suffer love.

"I will tell you the truth," says Alexander, but there is no dirt being crunched into his palm. The Dasein with the bowl raises it higher before Alexander to prompt his obedience, but still he refuses.

"Do you not have any respect for this court?" asks Nova sharply.

"I will give you my testimony, but I will not swear by some unintelligible thing that I stand on."

The Dublican's grin shows teeth now, and he is looking over at frustrated judges recoiling at the brute before them, for he is a thinking brute, but his thoughts unorthodox. As amusing as it is to watch the judges so easily perturbed by an upset tradition of these land dwellers, the Dublican is more interested in getting back to his station and speaks up for the judges in their stead, "Go on then, give us your account."

All three judges look at the Dublican with sour-onion looks. Alexander starts his story before they can challenge him further.

"My daughter fell into my arms last night, all bruised and bleeding. She had been raped," Alexander looks over at Parnassus, "by him!"

The Dasein shout more curses at Parnassus until they are ordered to be silent.

Sarasa is struck with horror and shows Anna her surprise.

"Why didn't you tell me?"

But tears are all she replies with.

"First my mother, and now you," Sarasa scoffs. She lets go of Anna's hand and disappears into the crowd.

Nova's eyes seem to be more concentrated on Alexander now.

"*Your* daughter?"

"Yes."

"*Yours?*"

"Anna is her name," says Alexander with a puzzled look. He can feel the red flame of anger jumping inside him as he understands why the judge makes him being a father a point to gawk at, and somehow, that point deserves more importance now than the fact of his daughter being raped.

"Where is this Anna?"

Alexander looks around the crowd for his daughter. A moment of silence suggests that he might be a liar.

"Well, where is she?"

"Anna," Alexander calls out, "it's okay."

Slowly and reservedly, Anna steps out of the crowd for all to see. She pulls her hood off, and with a clawed hand ensures her scar is covered by the red blanket of her hair. Nova beckons her to step forward, and she positions herself on the other side of her father so she does not have to see her rapist. Anna also gives only her word, and not with ceremony, and had the Dublican not been present, the proceedings might not have been as informative. The Dublican, likewise, jettisons past Anna's lack of oath ritual in order to expedite the trial. Anna affirms her father's story, concluding her statement with revealing the bite mark and bruising on her upper back.

"My child, you are still awaiting Kípos, are you not? Why do you wear a green tunic under a white robe?" asks Nova.

Anna is speechless. It is in that moment she realizes that it isn't tradition or religion or even belief that the Dasein resented, it is only that of *her* tradition, *her* religion, *her* faith. It is but a trifle of a detail to not wear the right color of tunic, but to the Dasein, it is a breach of tradition.

Anna gives pleading eyes to her incredulous father, and he speaks for her.

"She was raped! Her clothes ripped off her body! Her ceremonial attire is shredded. My God, listen to you!"

"Excuse me?" retorts Nova.

Alexander is sure that he will be sentenced to a Dead Land. The closest one to Biome 1 is a northern island in the Aegean Sea that the old world would have called Agios Efstratios. It is considerably larger than most Dead Lands, but the natural border of the sea seems an obvious location for a Dead Land. There is the home of old-world sympathizers, murderers, and sometimes those unfortunate to exceed the census counts of their biomes. There, unlucky Dasein would feast on fish and locusts for the remainder of their lives. Alexander now uses a bit of melodrama to harbor all of the attention so as to keep Anna from joining him on the Dead Land to dine with a mouth full of locust innards scraping against her teeth. He continues his rebuke.

"My daughter! That's right, *my* daughter stands before you, having to suffer the humiliation of exposing herself, of suffering this animal's presence once more," he says, pointing at Parnassus with his bound hands, "and you can't help yourselves but to delay justice because of the clothes she wears? Because I call her daughter? You know what? This is but a trifle compared to the greater issue I have with you. All of you!" Alexander looks around. He stops to look at the Dublican, sitting in front of him with a grin still sloping across his face. Alexander girds himself like a man and looks into the faces of the judges with rebuke flashing in his eyes. "You claim that Dasein is divine, and you proclaim this as if it were a new idea, something learned from the light of a secret sun, but it is not new. Many before you claimed the same sermon and preached it from their own esoteric traditions. Yours, theirs, all of it is a grave mistake. Divine, no, but royalty—yes. And we share in a royal charge from our creator to be His royal regents and stewards, caretakers of *His* earth. It seems you have felt it necessary to pedigree us as divine, and the earth also, in order to save all of creation. This was needless, for God made mankind a special tenant among all the other creatures when He personally blew into our lungs and looked into our faces in order to see His divine likeness. You all wanted to be just another animal, and look," he says, pointing again at Parnassus, "like animals you became."

"That is enough! You are done speaking," Nova commands. She wrinkles her face to show her contempt. "I have never heard, in all the years I have lived on this peninsula, such appalling talk. Your thoughts belong to a diseased mind. How this disease has not been discovered sooner is astounding. As for you, Parnassus, do you have anything to say for these charges against you?"

He lifts his fistful of dirt and lets it fall out slowly like the final granulates in an hourglass.

"Very well." After a couple minutes have passed with the Dublican and the judges conversing about the trial, Nova calls everyone to witness their judgment.

"All those who find Parnassus guilty of rape, cast your judgement."

All four of them pick up and throw a stone into the waters before them.

"All those who find Athos guilty of wrongful violence, cast your judgement."

All four throw stones.

"All those who find Athos guilty of false teachings, cast your judgement."

Four stones are heaved with fresh enthusiasm, such that both Anna and Alexander can feel the splash of the stones. The Dasein roar in delight. Frenzied shouting grows over them, and Anna witnesses the consequence of God-fearing conviction for the second time. Alexander's heart is as heavy as a tree stump still tethered to the earth by desperate roots. It is a tremendous weight, full of sorrow, but he has suffered the temptation for self-pity for as long as it takes him to cast his eyes on his daughter.

She flings her arms around him and cries. "Papa! Papa, no, no!" she cries out as the guards tear him away from her grasp.

"Anna! I love you!" is all he says. His sorrow will be for her only.

"Wait," calls out the Dublican, "Her, too." Anna feels hands grab her arms to restrain her.

"Why? What is it you want of me?"

"But you know why, don't you?"

"No," Alexander interjects. "You already have me. Allow me this act of bravery," he pleads, reciting Howard's own sentiments. Alexander's eyes search for sympathy but find only contempt.

Anna is so taken aback by the aggressive hold she is in, and the eagerness of it. It isn't she who is on trial. The Dublican walks coolly toward her with his hands behind his back after he smooths his suit down with the palms of his hands. He isn't physically superior to these land dwellers, but the haughty grin, the cocksure tone of his voice, the bemused look in his eyes; altogether poised like a chef's kiss. He is of absolute authority, and he knows it. Might does not make right in Biome 1, but he does.

Anna looks behind him to see the faces of the judges, hoping for some concern, but they have turned their backs and walked away. She feels gravity pulling her heart toward the earth.

"Let me go!"

The Dublican steps closer.

"Your cave is quite something. A little museum of ideas—isn't it?"

Anna's face flushes, and she becomes quiet.

"You know what happened to the museums? Gone! All of them. Yours will be too. But first thing's first: I am granting you an opportunity to decide how hard you want your life to be. Give up this toxic ideology your father has you dwelling on, and you'll remain living life abundantly here on Biome 1—or you can join your father in the Dead Lands. I'll give you the night to think it over."

Anna's bones rattle from that wise shiver that spare nothing but the threads of hair on her head. The rest of her body shakes under the cold night, which harasses and harbors the sleep from her eyes as she huddles on a table inside the round building in the heart of the monastery. She is locked inside, where she is to think over the Dublican's offer. It is dark inside the building. Moonlight yawns over the rooftops, but the surrounding monastery keeps most of the sleeping light from Anna's building. The midnight blue sky can be seen from an arched window up above, too high to climb out of, but it is where she looks when she prays.

"God … I want to love you, to honor you, but this world … they want nothing to do with you. They are forcing me to make a choice, and I'm scared to make it."

Anna's gaze falls, and she looks at the bottom of the door where light sneaks through, and she jerks back as if she's had an uncontrollable muscle spasm. The once slender blade of light on the ground is broken by two pillars of shadow. Anna slows her breathing so that she might hear what is on the other side of the door. She holds still so as to not creak the table and, for once, she forgets the cold biting at her feet. She waits.

A sound like mechanical spider legs, rusted and scratched, comes from the doorknob as it turns, and Anna begins to panic. It can't be time for an answer yet; the night still breathes serenely through the sky. The turning stops. It is locked, and whoever is on the other side doesn't have the key. But the two pillars of shadow remain under the door. A new sound comes, like fingers dragging along the door from top to bottom. This frightens Anna even more.

"Who's there?" she calls out.

"Anna. Anna, come to the door."

She can't make out the owner of the voice with the locked door between them. Anna stretches her cold body toward the door. The crack beside the door and the frame is not wide enough to see outside, and so she only has a voice to discern. Anna calls out again to see who is on the other side.

"It's your mother."

Antania stands outside of the door, garbed in the furl of the night. She wears shadows like a raven wears feathers, naturally.

Anna cannot respond. She is thankful for the door between them, if only to keep from her mother's stare; that is enough. But she will not speak, not until she knows what her mother wants with her.

"Anna, I know why you're in there. I know what you must choose. I came to help you."

"How could you possibly help me?" Anna scoffs.

"I could help you escape from here—to leave this place."

"Oh, so like how you helped Sybil with her child?" All Anna knows is what everyone else knows: that the child disappeared when The Crone intervened and only sometimes does her imagination land on the truth of it.

"Sybil sits as a queen; she is no widow or some other branded thing your father would have her be. And as for her child, it was doomed by the Dublican to go where you're looking to go. Don't you see, child, the world of men has been tamed, yet even now they remain dangerous. Chaos is in their blood. Come with me. Leave this place and live freely, as you would wish."

"Why do you even care?"

"You're not the only one who's been raped."

Anna can hear the difficulty in her mother's voice but can't decide whether it is because her mother hasn't been vulnerable with another in so long or if the truth about her mother is one that could be pitied and therefore a truth Antania labors at for dignity's sake.

"I was raped repeatedly by different men. They took turns. I know the pain you feel, Anna. It isn't merely a physical pain either. It injures your soul as well."

Antania's voice changes cadence a bit in order to tell a story.

"I wonder, do you know of the story of Medusa?"

"The woman with snakes for hair? Yeah, but why?"

"Well, you probably only know the bit when she became a gorgon, turning people into stone. She, too, was raped. She was raped by Poseidon in the temple of Athena. Like you, Medusa was exceedingly beautiful, such that she attracted the attention of gods as well. Many have thought that when Athena turned Medusa into a gorgon that it was a punishment for defiling her temple, but Athena was wiser than to give out punishment. She *gifted* Medusa with the ability to protect herself. You see, child, I am only offering you a way to protect yourself from the world and its monsters. If you come with me, you won't be caught in man's habit for chaos or abuse when the mood is just right for them. Is it not right that, as your mother, I should care for you? That I should want to protect you?"

Anna is stirred by her mother's words. All she really knows of her mother is that she did care about Anna's safety. In her own unique way, Antania wanted to protect her child and Anna can sense that is no lie. But there is something else that she can't ignore. Something so awful most of the Dasein on the peninsula ignore it. Anna needs to know.

"What ever happened to Sybil's child anyway?"

"Do you want out of here or not? We don't have time for this now. If you want to come with me, we need to go now. Anna!"

Antania's voice now whips through the door to prod Anna to be sensible, to be practical, to think of her own doom, but Anna is no fool. She intuits that her mother is as motherly as the earth. She suspects that her mother let the child die; somehow, this intuition is all she can think of, and her thoughts are crawling with spiders.

"Anna! If you're ready, we must go now!"

But Anna remains silent.

"Anna!" her mother hisses, sounding more like an angry cobra than a concerned mother.

Her mother continues, even tapping at the door, and this frightens Anna. She realizes that it isn't really about her. Her mother has come for some dark and invisible purpose, and so Anna begins to say aloud her favorite verse, over and over again.

"The Lord is my strength and my song; he has become my salvation … The Lord is my strength and my song; he has become my salvation …"

"Fool! You will die with the rest of the Patriarchy!" are the last words Anna hears from the other side of the door. Her mother leaves her there in tears and shadows.

THE CHANGELING

It is after the tears dried cold on Anna's face that she succumbs to fatigue. Her eyelids close the darkness out, and her mind hosts an alarming curiosity.

Anna walks barefooted over the cold earth. Night falls over her and some Dasein, standing, gazing into a pot of coals before her. The coals are steaming and piping incense into the air. As Anna walks closer, she can smell Bulgarian rose, sandalwood, and resin teeming in the air. It is delightful to her nose. It is a smell that is fit for a more genial time or lofty ceremony, but the phantasm of womanly eyes that look over the coals and up at Anna are now all-too familiar, and the insect of premonition thrums along her neck.

It is Antania but hooded with only coal black hair. She isn't adorned by bear skins, nor a twisting, climbing crown of forestry. She looks as Cleopatra would have on that snakebite night so many moons ago: eyes narrowed and with a determined look, set upon something dark, something deadly. Antania sticks a pointer finger toward Anna and signals with it for Anna to follow her through the thick fumes. Anna refuses to trail after her, watching her walk into a candlelit shelter; that is, until faces begin to give shape, clouding about her, moving toward her with nothing but teeth and eyes for Anna. Anna's heart dies and resurrects, over and over, giving her sporadic mobility in her legs as she follows. One-two-three-step, she dodges snarling and

*laughing faces. Four-five-six-step, she sinks her head down while slip-
ping past the other moaning, haunting ghouls fuming through the
air. Anna coughs through the haze that slithers into her nose, causing
her to be made more apparent to the faces chasing after her. She now
stands in front of a door where she's heard screams, loud and terrible.
She doesn't want to enter, but the faces …*

*She shuts the door to stave off the wild fiends grinning with violence
for her. She worries that the sound of the door will be heard once
her fear of the faces is left outside. Anna rushes into a small obscure
building made of stone walls with a female's wailing ricocheting off
of them. There, before Anna, are several shades of green veils across
the entry like a curtain. She doesn't want to lift a frayed edge and see
whatever the reason that causes this female to scream, but her hand
picks up from her side and Anna watches her hand lift the curtain
like a child watches a wind-up toy; curiously.*

*Before she peeks around the curtain, Anna hears another voice,
Antania's voice. Her voice is beckoning the other voice, "That's it,
keep going," she says.*

*Anna looks with need-to-know eyes and sees Sybil surrounded by
flickering candles that reveal her as sweaty, panting, and full-term.
It is an alarming vision. Sybil has always been snobbishly groomed
so that when Anna sees her hair disheveled, her face glistening in her
own sweat, and her skin blotchy, Anna cannot respond but with eyes
fixed. She has never seen a birth before, but the stomach clues her in
to what is going on. Perhaps more alarming yet is the sight of Antania,
seemingly normal. Her gentleness in the moment could trick anyone
else into the idea that she is compassionate, that she is benevolent.
Anna watches her as she dotes on Sybil, as she holds her hand and
prods her to push. She wipes at her forehead with a cloth and moves
her into different positions as she deems necessary—some allow for
comfort, others are to make use of the persistent nature of gravity.*

Anna does not move from the curtain she clings to. Without realizing it, she twists the curtain tight into her hands where all of her anxiety goes. Several hours have gone by, Anna unnoticed through all of them. She stands very still, making no sounds while engulfed in Sybil's anguish. Anna remembers to breathe only when Sybil is given the commands to push. Fortunately for her, the commands are now closer together. It isn't that Anna is so terrified by the look of it all, the sound of it all, but that she's indwelling in her the idea that somehow she is now witnessing a secret moment that has already transpired. The moment before Sybil became the Mother.

There is a change in Antania's tone, as if excited.

"That's it, you're almost there. Another big push," she says.

Sybil makes a final effort, a long and guttural sound issuing from her throat. The child's feet have now passed and are laying in cloths.

"Is it a—"

"A boy," Antania says coolly. "I will take care of it," she says as she gives a gentle squeeze to Sybil's hand.

Sybil turns her head away and doesn't say a word while Antania scoops up the child into her grasp. There is no celebration, no crescendo moment in the room, only the bizarre silence after so much labor. The child finally does cry out in self-awareness, causing Antania to move quickly. She wraps him up and turns, and upon turning around, she finally does see Anna standing there.

Anna is forgetting to breathe again. Being confronted by Antania's eyes, the child's cries swarming around them, and Sybil's strange silence, pandemonium surges in Anna's chest as she puts the pieces together to the puzzle the other Dasein only ever whisper at.

Antania looks over Anna's shoulder and gives a nod. Hands jut and clench on Anna's arms while Antania walks out with the child. Two other Dasein she does not recognize are gripping hard against her struggle, forcing her to stay in the room while Antania carries the boy off. Anna begins to cry as the child's cries become more distant.

"Get off of me! Let go!" Her cries turn to anger.

The Dasein let her go as they block the doorway and point to Sybil, suggesting that Anna should go to her. She looks at Sybil and sees her careened back with eyes closed, sweat and blood still clinging to her thighs. One-two-three-step, still no movement from Sybil. Four-five-six-step, her eyes still closed. Closer and closer she creeps until Anna stands over Sybil and looks her over before whispering her name.

"Sybil? Sybil, are you okay?"

Sybil's eyes, weak with exhaustion, open up to Anna's. Sybil leans forward and greets Anna with a smile. "Paidí mou," she says as she reaches for Anna and pulls her toward her until Anna's face lay against Sybil's bosom. "Paidí mou," she keeps saying, and does so while stroking fingers through Anna's hair.

Anna cries until she wakes.

THE BIGOT'S DAUGHTER

The carbon in the sky is rolling up the night while the morning's map lays over it to reveal a new world. The sun lifts beyond the zenith and flames the horizon violet and azure, pink and coral. The ombre sky is such that it can enchant the world alone, though many female Dasein silhouette against the peninsula like sun worshipers; their mystic's heart is less celestial: the Thrushes rise as if to sing the world into being.

It is an unintelligible song that reaches Anna's ears, and without select words or a confounding chorus, it could be decided—even by the Dublican—that their sound is beautiful. Their voices bewitching. Anna has risen early enough times to know that when the Thrushes sing like that, it is out of response to such a pretty sky, and she feels robbed of God's paintbrush. She can only see the patch of sky through the high window of the room, but it only offers the fading night.

It is not long after the Thrushes' song that the Dublican arrives. He opens the door, and morning pours into the building with an even more appalling vision than her father all bruised and bloodied. The Dublican looks past the room's storage of ceremonial elements—tinctures of bay leaves, newly hung thistle blossoms, juniper berries swaddled in cheesecloth—and he sees a huge black cross etched into the wall behind Anna. He looks at her with an aghast expression and sees blackened fingers hanging by her side. She is unflinching, and her gaze pierces with what looks to him as utter contempt. He studies her brave look and thinks of his ex-wife, and this angers him so. He is feverishly mad, and his thoughts come out in starts and turns.

"Why, look at this ... Why, you just didn't ... did you?" Realizing his excited and emotional demeanor, the Dublican collects himself by smoothing his suit with the palm of his hand and breathing deeply through his nose.

"I thought I could show you my answer instead," replies Anna. She'd found some charcoal that would have been otherwise used in a ritual, and this knowledge puts a tinge of a smile at the corners of her mouth. The cross stands large, as tall as she could reach while standing on the table she huddled on all night. He sees it as a spiteful image, and the Dublican feels provoked by it.

"You think this is funny? I'm not done with you just yet." The Dublican turns and is pulling the door behind him, but before he closes it, he gnashes at her: "We'll see just how much humor you have when I'm through with you." And he slams the door behind him.

Night is wholly retreated by the time Anna receives another visitor. She is surprised to have in front of her a dress-wearing Sybil. Sybil wears a fringe halter-like crop top that lattices in the middle in order to expose a double portion of her breasts with a crocheted dress that falls to her calves. She looks like the muse of Troy.

"You look cold," says Anna, who could see erect nipples through Sybil's meager morning attire.

"So do you." Anna is clutching at the white robe she wears over her green tunic. The night's cold had gotten into her bones, and she can't get warm in the dimly lit building.

"Paidí mou, what have you done?" asks Sybil while looking at the tremendous charcoal cross. But Anna will not answer; instead, she deliberately looks away from Sybil, hoping that she will take the hint. "Oh, Anna, my dear, you are scared—that's what this is all about. Scared of your own freedom and what you might do with it. I know, I was scared too. The possibilities! To be in control of your own priorities, your own values, your own identity—it was almost too much to bear, but your mother, she showed me the way." Anna turns and stares at Sybil with a surprised look. "Sarasa told me."

Anna wants to be angry at Sarasa for breaking her promise, and for leaving her in the crowd, but even now she can't. She feels pity. She feels sorry for her.

"Paidí mou—"

"I am not your child!" Anna interrupts. It seems easy for her to do because of the despisal she feels toward Sybil for her selfish ways masked as benevolence. There are fictions more faithful, more virtuous than her. Sybil is more of a Helen of Troy than a Penelope of Ithaca. "You are not my mother!" Anna continues. "Neither is that witch you look up to." Anna's dream is still fresh in her mind. The dilemma of whether to commit social suicide no longer gnaws at her. She does not dismiss the strange possibility that she is unwittingly able to peek into a secret history, but she has accepted its truth. A truth she cannot ignore. "I know about the child. The boy you gave birth to."

"How is it you know this?" asks Sybil. Only she and Antania knew the child's sex. Sybil steps nearer while studying Anna carefully.

"I also know that you gave him up. You gave him away to that *witch*! You let him be carried off, still warm from your womb, without so much as a name. Do you even know what she did with the child?"

The question turns rhetorical as Sybil stares back, matching Anna's incredulity, and for once, Anna feels a justified superiority.

"Do you have any idea what awaits you?" asks Sybil. She does so with a flash of anger never before seen; it almost seems a new expression, seems contrived, but so does the rest of her. She goes on, "I came here to sway you away from such a foolish choice. You will lose everything, perhaps your very life."

"You should pay more attention to your own daughter. Her life is more delicate than you realize."

Sybil seems to ignore this remark. "So, that's it then? You will choose to stay and wait for condemnation rather than walk out of here with me into the beautiful spring day? Paidí mou, your freedom is out there," she says, pointing out the door. She glances at the cross behind Anna once more. "Fathers ruin children, there is no doubt. I am sorry for you, my dear. I'm sorry that you'll never know true freedom. I would have killed my own father if I knew such freedom existed. Well, enough of such words. You're as ugly as your tongue, they say."

Anna watches the golden-haired goddess walk toward the door. Sybil lingers at the door to smell the carbon outside, her eyes closed as she does so, and speaks aloud, "Blessed be, what a fine day it is." The door closes behind Sybil and shuts Anna in once more.

A world without memory is a world of being, of the present, of moments. Can such a world as Anna's even think of the past?

Anna was a girl, and she had a father who loved her very much, but would the peninsula remember the girl, the only girl to have a father on Biome 1? "What a strange Dasein he was," they might say and, "Such a poor girl, fooled to think like her father." To think outside of the circle of Antania's magic, beyond the alluring canvas of Sybil's body, or even greater than the Dublican's dreams of a new and far off planet was not a simple calculus of heresy, but an unsanctioned fanaticism that threatened the sustainability, the diversity, the plurality of worlds that exists in the minds of the Dasein.

Anna thinks of Stephanos. She remembers how brave he was in the end, how he looked at her as if to say, "It's okay." That it was okay that her father had lied to the invading Dasein, telling them that they were tourists who'd bribed the monks to stay. She remembers the delicate look he gave—the gentleness, the kindness with which his eyes shone. She wonders if he'd planned this lie with her father or not. She wonders what would have happened if the truth was told that day. How many years of life would they have cut short? Was the lie worth all her present sufferings?

Alexander is locked away in the Dublican's quarters in a spare room where he'd stayed all night. It is a small but curious room. It must have been a lounging room where Howard did much thinking because Alexander stares at a wall graffitied with molecular structures of many things. Red wine's chain stretches long beside caffeine's; a doodle of a steaming cup above its structure and a glass of red above its structure are how Alexander discerned them. A wall riddled with hexagons and tick marks and O's and C's and H's and numbers. Dozens and dozens of hexagons are strewn across the wall, and the shape of them strikes his mind familiar. They stand out like a great honeycomb latticed large with letters loitering like bees.

Alexander's physical surroundings may have been a bit more hospitable, with the sofa underneath him, the temperate air that swirls above him, and a small circular window for gazing across the sea, but he nonetheless tossed and rocked and fidgeted all night. He sits on the sofa in the morning with night still under his eyes and gazes at the wall. Its intelligence is lost on him. Alexander can think only of Anna and fears for her many possible outcomes, all of them tragic.

After the Thrushes' song, and when morning shadows had begun to shift, that's when he hears the Dublican's voice sounding deliberate and commanding. He can tell that he is outside, and apparently other Dasein are with him taking orders from him. Alexander can hear several males heaving something very large occasionally thudding and scraping against the Dublican's station. It is the only moment Alexander does not dwell fearfully but thinks wonderingly. He wonders what can have prompted the Dublican to invite more Dasein to his station. He despises them all. Whatever his purposes, Alexander knows it must be imperative.

He thinks of his daughter once more.

The key difference between the victim and the guilty is action. Had Anna relinquished all her energies to effect recognition of God, and yet still her secret heart was found out, perhaps she would be a victim. Instead, she stood before the Dublican, guilty. Guilty of ideology rather than victim of faithfulness.

Anna looks at the metallic chamber that has been hauled inland by the Dublican's working party, now turned audience to witness the path of the righteous. What a strange and surreal occasion it is: she, surrounded by male Dasein, who live by the conviction that labors to sustain freedom of earth and female alike; and even her father stands there, and all of them under a noonday sun. And while Alexander does stand with ropes about his wrists, she feels a prick of anger toward him. Angry as she thinks that instead it should be him to get the chamber rather than her. He'd brought her to the peninsula, after all. It was he who'd brought her this heinous fate. Anna is thinking along these rough currents, skirting across victimhood's shores, while she looks at her father, seeing the crab of shame crawling all over his face; and had she continued to look on him, she would have begun to entertain her mother's ideology about fathers and men.

Anna's eyes fall from her father's face, and she sees a milk thistle on the ground, not yet molested, untouched by wandering livestock. Its bloom is pink, and while it cheats the idea of beauty to the local Dasein, Anna is not convinced. She stares at it for some time, and her thoughts turn to Stephanos once more. It was on her seventh birthday that he'd introduced Anna to her favorite flower. She remembers picking the flower with angelic-like petals out of a large, wrinkled hand. It made his hand look like a snow-covered summit sitting in his palm. Stephanos had given her her first snowdrop flower and a smile that couldn't be seen underneath his great stringed beard but was noticed at the creases made by his eyes. She remembers the day with delighted fondness.

"Do you know the story of the snowdrop?" asked Stephanos while presenting the flower to Anna.

She shook her head of red curls side to side.

"There was a monk who lived by himself here on the mountain. He worked by himself, he took bread by himself, he remained always by himself. The other monks let him be, seeing that was his preference. He only ever came near to the others for mail, for he wrote letters, and often. But the letters would stop coming."

"Why did they stop?"

"Well, he wrote to his father. His father died. Cancer, leaving him with no one to write to."

"How sad. I don't think I like this story."

"Oh, but it gets better, my dear, I promise."

Little Anna gave the old monk a peppery look of doubt. Stephanos contended her stare with a rascally expression, which succumbed to an honest chuckle.

"Shall I continue?" Anna raised her chin and turned her face to look at him with only one eye, for that's all she needed to warn him with. "As I was saying, this monk was now the only one left in his family. He felt terribly alone. His days were filled with work, but the nights haunted him with sorrow until one day … oh, well you probably don't want to hear the rest," he said as he turned his head away slightly and peeked at Anna from the corner of his eye.

"You must! You can't stop now! You said it would get better, you promised."

"Oh well, if I must." Stephanos smiled. "The monk was so saddened, and felt so defeated, that he wandered up the mountain in the middle of February, looking for a spot to jump. It was so cold that one's breath could be seen, and snow still remained on the upper reaches of the mountain. He didn't care though; he had enough of his sadness."

"Did he jump?"

"He found the place where he would, but in a great wrestle with his mind against his heart, he decided to pray. But he didn't just pray, he screamed, hoping that God would hear him. If it was going to be his last prayer, he thought he better speak up, and so he did. He yelled, scaring all of the birds away as he did, saying, 'God, give me a sign! Tell me that he's all right, that he's with you!'

he said. The monk waited. He listened for a good while, but there was no word. He fell down on a patch of snow and sobbed. The monk's tears had wet the snow below him just enough for him to notice a green shoot that was below the surface. It confused him because there shouldn't have been anything so green and vibrant at the time. He immediately had it in his mind to dig and find out what it was."

"It was the flower."

"Yes, but it was more than that. To the monk, it was an answer from Heaven. He never saw a snowdrop flower before that moment. To find something alive under something that smothers life was, in his mind, a gentle answer from God. At once, he picked the flower up from the ground and brushed it off to see it fully. He stepped away from that high place and carried the flower down the mountain and told the other monks all that had happened making this flower," Stephanos was now raising the flower in his hand, "the most cherished flower on the peninsula, for it kept the monk from hopelessness. It is a symbol of hope during difficult seasons." Stephanos finished his story and gave Anna the snowdrop. She didn't realize it then, but in that moment, she loved him like a grandfather.

"Anna!" The Dublican's voice is now louder than her thoughts. "What will it be? Your father's ideals or a free and thriving life?" The Dublican's voice is sharp, his words blunt, but his face seems amused at the ultimatum. For him, the question is easy and flows out of his mouth like an early morning wind. For her, the question feels like she is caught in a tempest. He grins at her with a triumph that only an apex predator can know. If he were a lion and she the prey, it would be just seconds before his deadly assault. But she will not be easy prey.

"Your question," she starts, "suggests that all of my art, which you found, is nothing more than a regurgitation of my father's mind." Anna proceeds to move her hair so that her whole face can be seen. Slow and deliberate, she will make herself known publicly for the first time. "What you saw, Dublican, was my ideology. My faith. My thoughts. If you're gonna punish me, at least give me the courtesy of ownership."

The Dublican hasn't seen such brazen speech since his wife. The certainty, the boldness, the supposed triumph in the moment appalls him, rendering him speechless. He gives her a quick smile but makes a long and concentrated effort to smooth his hands down his suit. He requires a moment to collect his thoughts. He fears being rash and retorting with emotion. He is a scientist, after all. He is supposed to be the objective one, not as some land dweller riddled with emotion. The only thing that he will let influence his carbonic mind, at least in front of other Dasein, is his status as Dublican and Liaison of Biome 1.

The Dublican turns directly to Alexander, and his smile leaves him; his face becomes stoic while he proceeds to describe the chamber and its effects on its occupants.

"Allow me to educate you on this chamber you see behind me. The chamber is made of brass, sheet metal, and aluminum metal foam. The brass and sheet metal allow for electromagnetic shielding to disrupt the magnetism of the earth, which, in turn, inhibits the Dasein from feeling it. The aluminum foam is present to absorb any residual energy, ergo rerouting the magnetic flux." The Dublican can see that Alexander is uneasy when he is detailing the chamber's features, but he isn't yet satisfied. He wants to torture Alexander like the Dublican's wife tortured him with her many-years absence. He steps closer toward Alexander and now speaks so that only he can hear. "Your daughter will be given a paralytic that will steal away her ability to feel anything. She will be lowered into water that has a highly concentrated amount of salt to allow her body to buoy, granting her the sensation of a gravityless environment. She will be locked inside without light or sound. All of her senses will be taken from her. She will turn deaf, dumb, and mute, and the longer she stays in there, the more she will doubt her own existence. Your daughter may go mad right before your eyes. And when she has had enough time in there, I will open the door and let the witches reacquaint her to your primordial ancestor—Earth."

Anna watches her father made nervous by the Dublican's words. It always seems an odd occasion when her father is speechless, and she begins to worry when he objects to whatever the Dublican tells him and seeks her place in the chamber instead. The bizarreness of the moment seems capitalized by her male audience and servants to the Dublican. It is like a cult of reason has come to make another convert, and it is she who is to be initiated by some heinous challenge.

The Dublican commands for Anna to be brought closer to the chamber. The Dasein obliges his caesarian-like authority and clutches at her arms and pushes her toward the chamber. The Dublican opens it by a control panel on the face of it, and a great hissing sound issues from its airtight locks. Its foreignness of sight and sound alarms even the Dasein serving the Dublican—to whom he nods and motions toward Anna, reminding them to seize her. The Dublican holds in his hand a needle with the paralytic solution in its tube and raises it in front of Anna's face.

"Last chance," he says. "What's it gonna be?"

She gives him no words, no tears, only a steadfast look, and with both eyes visible.

"Such foolish confidence." The Dublican grabs Anna's wrist and pulls it tight while the needle pricks her arm. Anna sees a smirk growing on the Dublican's face while she feels the push of the numbing agent enter her veins. She stares long at the Dublican's face and wonders at this bizarre summons on her behalf. It is she who was raped, assaulted, and already a sufferer of criminal activity now made to suffer like a criminal of the most scandalous kind: As a traitor with bigoted counselors whose ideas need only to be smothered before its fire turns wild. Her dismayed look peels away from the face of her judge as she begins to feel the paralytic robbing her limbs. Anna falls forward into the Dublican's arms, and he lowers her to the ground.

"It's working," he says. "Come, you two, grab her and get her inside."

Anna can't move at all save for the rise and fall of her chest. She can't feel the warmth of the sun above her nor the grit of the earth below her. She can still hear at the present, and she hears her father yelling, over and over, that he loves her. He sounds frenzied, and his helplessness becomes obvious by his repetitions. At first, they are with reassuring promise, but eventually they seem as claims full of pain and despair. This brings tears at the corners of her face until they stream unknown into her ears, forming tiny pools. Not even she would hear her cries that day.

The Dublican supervises Anna being lowered and eased into the pool of salts until he is sure she floats without aid. The Dasein step away at the Dublican's command, and he stares down at her bobbing on her back, her hair fanning out pretty like a submerged petal; but her beauty is not enough to dismay the grin etched on his face. He feels no remorse, no pity, nor the empathy perpetuated for Dasein-kind, for species, for the flora and fauna of ecosystems. She lies there, not as a Dasein worthy of protection and rights, but as an idea to prune from her father's eyes. The Dublican touches the control panel in order to dictate the time to allot for her punishment.

Anna tries to blink but cannot. The sun streams onto her face with indifference whenever the Dublican moves his shadow. Once he stands back up, he peers down at her, and he appears as if an eclipse. There isn't a cloud in the sky, but the Dublican's head produces enough shadow over her when he gazes upon her that she feels the dread of night closing in fast around her. She can no longer hear the pitiful declarations of love from her father. The water comes just above her ears, muffling all sound, and just short of her eyes to dab away at fresh tears. She lies there surrounded by the green and white hues of her garments. Not a shutter or ripple across the watery confinement, just a pair of eyes under that saffron hair confronting the shadow that stares back. At last, the door is shut and the darkness swallows Anna whole.

It is perfect darkness. Its virtue rendered by the effect: a darkness felt, as if it were a presence, but without shape or form or face to peer into. Anna is smothered by it. It is a dungeon of nothingness, as if the Dublican had found the keys to Tartarus and locked her in. Yet even Tartarus contained some few condemned to make company with and a dark lord to gawk at. She has neither. She feels her mind and nothing else, and in her mind, she clamors against the unrespiting dark. She is without flame or luminating source, without sun or moon or stars. Even the darkest of nights holds more light than that chamber. Forms could still be found, shadows seen, and distance discerned, but not there. Anna is wreathed under a great shadow, as if by eternal night. If there is ever a way to discern the universe in its embryonic stage, the chamber provides such means.

Anna lies there where time and space are but fictions, and all of the contents of her mind are now weighed only by the proofs of her anecdotal life now hiding in the recesses of her brain. She thinks of her father's view on light once more: *Without it, there is no art.* Her heart beats with love, then with great distress. Time is always discerned by light, by the blaze of a single star. She cannot tell how long she lies in there like a brain in a vat. And the silence … that silent night of her demise causes her thoughts to sprint toward and away from panic. But it is not silence entirely. The quiet looms over her, making the chamber seem more vast than it is, but the quiet offers the stage to the sound of her heartbeat concussing into the briny waters and back into her ear canal. She hears when her lungs expand and deflate, and the air circulating in and out of her nostrils seem as wind tunnels that disappear into the cave of her chest. The silence gives more exaltation to her body than the dark does, but it only exploits how alone she is in that torture chamber. Oh, how she wishes for just one star, something to look at, something to reference besides her pining thoughts under numbed flesh. But hers is an uncharitable universe, and the verse spoken is not, "Let there be light." It speaks nothing of carbon either, but instead renders it myth. Yet, like the parallel universe she came from, myths transcend.

There is no vacancy for carbon's crafty ideologies, its excellence, its many functions. The chamber speaks lies about the light with wicked taunts, and with invisible smile, that sunless chamber seems triumphant. Anna closes her eyes so as to keep the whites of them from being swallowed too. It feels better to pretend one is dreaming terrible dreams than to see the face of sin so close to hers. The thought of being thrust into a mighty storm where thunderbolts and Jupiter-sized clouds would collide with great violence seems a more pleasant scene, for at least there would be variant hues of fire and smoke and cumulus skies and many great and terrible focal points where fear could be grasped. She feels the emptiness of light's absence and finds nothing. She is nowhere. Gone.

Anna gives thought to the fact of her ability to close her eyes, and she is at once excited and frantic. She keeps them closed but moves her eyes side to side with new-found movement. She realizes the paralytic is slowly beginning to wear off, and it gives her more will to overcome the darkness. She can't yet feel the salty liquid against her face but is now able to squint her eyes, which flex along the bridge of her nose. She gives a focused effort to draw breath in from her nose, hoping to smell something, anything. The nothingness also smells like nothing, staving off her hopes to defeat the vastness of nothing. She wrinkles her face some more as best she can until she feels tears by her eyelashes, cold and wet.

An hour has passed over Alexander's head, all the while he stands watching his daughter in motionless torment. He doesn't trust the science of the process and readies himself to somehow intervene should Anna begin to sink in the water.

"Anna, can you hear me? Anna, just hold on. I'm right here. Anna? Anna?"

"She can't hear a word you're saying," says the Dublican.

The Dublican spends more time studying Alexander's face than Anna's, savoring his torture, every mournful bend at his forehead, every painful wince in his eyes. There is a private joy and a self-realized omnipotence in the moment. But he is a just god, if there ever was one—so go his thoughts on the matter.

"Nah, she can't hear a single thing you're saying right now. Nothing but the sound of her blood networking to and fro through her body. She's in there listening to the droning sound of her pulse. It's just her and the chamber. She's in there experiencing the universe before the big bang. It's just her consciousness up against a blackboard of utter nothingness." He says his last remark with a peculiar satisfaction like he's tasted a delicious morsel of sweet chocolate when he shouldn't have. If he had, you would be able to see the dark stains in his teeth as he gives Alexander a big toothy grin.

Alexander is instantly filled with rage, leaps for the Dublican, and reaches for him with bound hands. The Dublican leaps backward while his faithful horde of land dwellers restrain Alexander once more. Hands grab at his wrists and arms and neck, thrusting him backward and away from the just god of Biome 1. Alexander snarls like a beast and grunts through the choking hands until the Dasein restraining him feel confident in their strength. Alexander yells insults to the Dublican's ears instead of landing blows to his eyes.

"God damn you! Damn you all! It would be better if this place were burned to ash and sown with the salts of your limbs!"

"There it is," chimes the Dublican. "That's the Christian spirit the world loved so much. Don't you see," he now speaks to the Dasein, "this fellow is a contagion, and his true face is now revealed. Lord only knows what true face hides behind those red curls in there," he says, pointing at the chamber. The Dublican smiles big until he sees that Alexander realizes the irony in his last remark. The Dublican enjoys his wit, his lived-knowledge of both pre- and post-Old World War, his station, his ability to enact vengeance on behalf of all who'd suffered the religious—even the tiniest of offenses, like the moral snobbery founded in a grim and disappointed stare: The Dublican is now arbiter and bringer of justice for all who were wronged by church or mosque or temple, and more than a little did the past inform his present judgments. The Dublican feels reciprocal rage, as if the furies of Alexander's thoughts stir the waters of his mind into a turbulent passion, the mad maestro reappearing. The Dublican approaches Alexander with quick steps and grabs his hair like a mophead, pulling him closer to the chamber, the land dwellers standing close by in the event of a brawl.

"Look at her!" he says as he thrusts Alexander's face only millimeters from the chamber screen. "Look! You see that? That is all your doing. You caused this. Think real hard about this situation before you go condemning me. You know the regulation! And so does she!"

Alexander looks at her with a wet face, his eyes dampened by a father's love. His failure seems complete, and the weight in his throat confirms it so. A father is supposed to protect his children. He could not protect Anna from this danger, not forever. He watches as she now lies entombed, surrounded by utter darkness, squirming her head around and all in a fit. She looks like a child plagued by nightmares with no one to console her, and this brings an ache in his stomach. A guttural noise bellows out from his mouth to give sound to the pain of a helpless parent. His face wrinkles with agony. He cries aloud and pleads for it to stop.

Sinner before the judge crying mercy.

"Have mercy, please. Stop this. Let me complete her allotted time."

"Mercy is a religious term. That word no longer exists. There's nothing in nature that is merciful. I don't know what you speak of." The Dublican now takes on the airs of a dignified scientist whose time is worth more than any land dweller could afford.

"There's nothing natural about any of this!" says Alexander, looking to the chamber.

Tears trek down and out of the troughs that once held them. Alexander has the look of the pitiful writ across his face, but the bound wrists do not help his cause, for he looks like a criminal as well. The Dublican stares at him until he is at once distracted and his gaze pulls away from Alexander to a vision that skirts across the horizon behind him. Alexander notices the Dublican's eyes beam over his shoulder; he follows them and sees a vessel making a fast approach to the peninsula.

"Ah, well, they haven't wasted any time, have they?" asks the Dublican. He looks back to Alexander, "You know that boat is for you, right?"

"I don't care! Please, just get my daughter out of that chamber."

"I think you'll appreciate the effort I put in to get you sent to a special location."

"Please! The chamber!"

"Or would you rather it a surprise?"

The Dublican laughs with such amusement that the land dwellers now recognize the subjective nature in him. He's shown the ribbed underbelly of someone who gets tickled by the pain of others. But it isn't until he sees *her* that he realizes this quality exists in him. His embarrassment is only in that others could now see it too.

She stands under the shade of a pine tree with a hood draped over her head, and her eyes pierce through the dark soot that borders them.

"It's you," mutters the Dublican.

Antania remains still, and her gaze does not leave him. She is about ten meters away, but her presence is felt as if within a blade's reach of his throat. The Dublican's demeanor changes remarkably upon seeing the Crone with her eerie look about her, making a very public display of herself. It is the first time he has seen her in person. All other occasions had only been recorded on his drone footage, and there is no fright to be had when looking at an infrared version of her moonlight journeys. There she is, in the flesh, and with deliberate intent to be seen by him.

The Dublican walks over to the ungodly chamber and promptly types in a sequence that initiates a jolt, followed by a hissing sound from the locks. He looks back toward the pine tree, but Antania is gone. He is at once relieved and annoyed by this. He cannot understand the psychology of it, of how she commanded fear with a simple stare, and the fact that he would fear her at all troubles him.

Alexander takes an eager step toward the chamber upon seeing the door open, and the Dublican quickly rebukes him for it.

"Wait! All of you! She cannot be released so quickly from the chamber. She's been without her senses for a while; she will need a moment." He turns to Alexander again saying, "Hopefully she's found her senses now."

They pull her out slowly from the pool of tears and shadows. Anna can feel Dasein hands with hers. Her skin reports the warm sensation of sunlight, and it is as a gentle kiss on the face, but her eyes are shut like clams. She can see the light with eyes closed already, and it is a new kind of blindness, but she welcomes it like a fond memory. She cannot yet feel her legs, and the Dasein assisting watch them buckle under her until she lies on the earth as a newborn, disoriented and helpless.

"Idiots! She cannot feel her feet yet due to the curbed timing of her confinement. Pick her up!" she hears the Dublican say. It isn't much in the way of a greeting or consoling phrase, but she welcomes the sound of his voice all the same. She crunches the dirt beneath her between her fingers and feels its grit once more. She can smell the ocean teeming with the scent of herbs and wild-flowers and pine dancing through her nose. She fidgets with her hands together some more, feeling the dirt against the prune flesh of her fingers, her eyes still closed and breathing in suspicious slow breaths.

"You see that?" she hears the Dublican say. "It's as if she's new to the earth once more. It was approximately an hour and a half occupation time. Not even two hours, and look, that's what becomes of it."

"Anna? Anna? I'm here. Please, talk to me." She hears her father sounding anxious and decides she should try opening her eyes again, but the light is too much for her—as if a recipient of rebuke, she is subdued by objective reality.

Alexander, while privy to all his senses, feels like he, too, is losing them. His panic, teeming with his guilt, tugs his heart wildly as if he's been standing in a purgatory of a kind. He feels burdened by thoughts like, *Will she give up on me? On God? Will she stay? Is this our last meeting place? Why didn't we leave this place long ago? How could I be so complacent to allow this? Lord forgive me.*

The Dublican resumes his bias and continues in his pretended lordship. He hails her to stand before him again, and by Dasein hands, she stands.

"Look at you now. So full of riddles, I'm sure. You must think me cruel. The both of you!" The Dublican looks over his shoulder at Alexander and glares at him. "Don't you see? This is your last chance—such chances don't exist in nature. I'm giving you one last opportunity, Anna. Now choose! Your father or this biome?"

Anna squints through the afternoon light. She looks beyond the Dublican's frenzied stare, past her father's sorrowful look, and out toward the two eternities: blue, beaming, and blithe. But it is no longer a background she adores, if the foreground is to be the peninsula where time ticks atheist by day and pagan by night. She would rather look to God's paintbrush over some other horizon, bristled or spattered, it didn't matter. She thinks of Stephanos and of how he might have shared a like-musing in his final ultimatum. Anna staggers, trying to stand on her own, and when realizing she can't yet, she flexes the upper reaches of her spine so as to appear taller before responding. Her face patient. Her eyes resolute.

"I must go get ready to leave with my father," she says. Her voice is calm and without a hint of a sting or injury to her health: her final affront.

The Dublican is furious. He's counted on her recanting her painted glories and rejecting her father. When he looks at Anna, all he can see is the woman he married, who'd recanted his materialist world and rejected him for all but a single turn around the sun to revel in her theology full of labors and strife. He looks at Anna, who also seems to prefer death over a free and abundant life won by so many heroes, and he knows now that there is no amount of calculus or logic to turn her face from certain death.

"You are as stupid as your father then. You would trade this bit of earth, this utopian dream dreamt of and pined for by so many before you? And for what? To be called woman? Man? The world your father has taught you subjects you and enslaves you. In that world, you are a second-rate citizen. In every class, in every culture, every faith dared to shackle women to a lesser station and dull women's dreams to the practical whims of some capricious yet pretended virtue of a man. What some called courage should have only ever been called greed. Their lusty appetites for land or wealth or enterprise fueled their intentions with pretenses of courage and daring, but in truth it was greed. Once a man got his desired lot, he wreathed himself righteous. That, my dear, is the world you are going back to." Like his wife once did, Anna returns a steadfast look full of contentment, no matter the perilous road before her.

The Dublican once more turns toward her father and sneers at him. "That island out there," he says, pointing to the sea, "you're not going to it. You and your daughter will be going on a little trip across the Mediterranean, to the Kidron Valley. A perfect location for the kind of diseased minds you have. What do you think about that?"

"People used to pay handsomely to be buried there; I'll get in for free. I think I'm getting a bargain deal out of it," says Alexander.

"Parnassus! He goes too! Let's see how your Christianity plays out then."

The Dublican looks at his team of land dwellers and speaks fitfully to them saying, "Come! Let's get these two ready for pickup. And go get, Parnassus! Hurry! Their disease might be catching."

Alexander lets himself feel momentous joy despite Anna's sealed fate. She looks courageous to him, and he feels a father's pride in his child. She has taken as many assaults and insults these Dasein could give her. Cast doubt and incited fear in the most heinous ways, but still she remains true. She has outdone her father, and in that moment, he can't help but to return her stare with a look of adoration. He kisses at his fingertips and moves his hands toward her in a way he'd done when she was a child, and the two shared the last occasion of fathers and daughters the peninsula would see.

The land dwellers, all, could not imagine where Anna had been nor where she would go. Those albatross sails that fluttered after her came with prodigious speed and would make her invisible; like carbon dioxide she went. The peninsula exhaled them both: like daughter like father, they were whisked away and removed from the biome like the invasive species they were.

As evening drew near, Antania stood gazing like she always does in the twilight ticks before her pagan moon tocks, but it was not with the same delight and savor as all the moons before. A tear borne out of anger cascaded down her face, and she wiped away its evidence as if the other night birds would shriek at her if they saw it. She was moved by so much hate. She had lost Anna before, but it was as a mother. She suffered the loss yet again, but it was not by a mother's heart that beat in her chest this time. She was the Crone. It was in that moment she realized that, despite all her authority, all of her prestige, she still fell prey to a man and that the Free World had yet to be free of male dominion after all.

She was panting for breath now as she thought murderous thoughts of all the intricate ways she could end the Dublican's reign and his very life made to fall under her darkness. She let out a screeching sound full of terrible agony, which echoed across the peninsula once she determined to pull the Dublican into the deep dark abyss that awaited them both, for darkness is neither male nor female, but an androgynous host whose purpose it is to steal and thoroughly rob them of all identity, till there's nothing left of them but stillborn thoughts.

AFTER

At week's end, the Dublican had completed his maintenance on his troubled drone and was making it ready for flight. He smoothed its feathers down over the on/off switch and proceeded out the door of his station so he could jet it into the air before tending his bees on the shore. As he stepped out, he saw a vision that alarmed him. A human skull sat staring at him from the ground, its dead face indifferent to his alarm.

Much to Antania's delight, she watched the Dublican slowly reach for it and canvas about, looking for the one who'd delivered it. She watched him go back inside.

It became a game of chess between Antania and the Dublican. Queen to C-Eight, takes bishop. The Dublican had already sacrificed his queen to the war he'd waged against humanity. He was now cornered and without his pawns.

The Queen of Darkness now advanced toward checkmate. Not even daylight would get in her way now.

In the end, carbon's lust over human life is ever a tragedy, its lonely passion marked by how desperate it clings, even to the bones remaining.

There is yet any sign of carbon's necromancy concerning the lives of Alexander or Anna. Together they stand beside an ancient ravine that cuts the earth jagged and from it lift foul odors. The stream moves a slow trickle that crawls like a snake shedding its skins from so much refuse and neglect.

As refuse and neglect, Anna and her father stand in the Dead Land of the Dublican's choosing. It is a foreign land to Anna and Alexander. A land that has suffered the rage of some foreign war that turned many monuments desolate and austere.

There is still one not yet debilitated, which from Tradition's tongue has been called, "Absalom's Monument." Beyond it, outstretched and many, are the graves of the sons and daughters of Abraham as wide as many fields. Some of those stones are dashed to pieces, others flung from their corpse, one of many affronts to the people of the Image once born.

Together, they look over the stream, upward to the great walls surrounding; still higher, to the battlements of what was once the Holy City latticed against the morning sky.

Alexander and Anna have been delivered into the Valley of Shadow and Death, where they still yet hope for the miraculous and idyllic image of God.

ABOUT THE AUTHOR

He is a poet at heart, a philosopher in mind, and an artist in spirit. When he's not trying to draft the sequel to this book, he can be found chasing his son around the house, falling prey to his wife's excellent cooking, or smoking cigars with the dog. He lives in the Central Texas area with his wife, Katy, his son, Henry, and their dog, Bonnie.